Blaine Harrigan stood there, wearing a light jacket now and holding a potted red gerbera daisy.

"To brighten a windowsill," he said with a smile. "I take it your new boss is happily sleeping?"

Just seeing him drew a bright smile from her and a rush of warmth. Man, she didn't even know this guy. It was too soon to be happy to see him, wasn't it?

Heck, she didn't care. It was nice to see him, to feel as if she might have made her first friend here. She stepped back, inviting him in.

"Thank you for the daisy. I just love it. What a kind thought." She looked at the bright flower with a sudden feeling of comfort, as if she weren't a total stranger here anymore. "I was thinking about making some tea. Would you like some?"

"I never turn down a cuppa," he answered. He handed her the flower and she motioned him to follow her to the small kitchen and dining area. She placed the daisy on the sill over the sink, then turned to find him standing in the doorway, evidently awaiting an invitation to sit or go.

* * *

CONARD COUNTY: THE NEXT GENERATION

Dear Reader,

Babies can bring us some of the most joyous times in our lives. In this story, Diane has been given her cousin's newborn child to care for, and she's totally unprepared. Who wouldn't be, when they've never had or even babysat a child? In addition, within days of accepting the baby, she starts a new job as an urban planner in Conard County. A lot to handle all at once.

She finds the most unexpected ally in Blaine Harrigan, the county engineer. He's an Irishman who helped raise a bunch of younger siblings, so he's an old hand with tiny people. What's more, he even likes them, and surprises Diane by how quickly a man can come to care for an infant. She would have expected him to run.

As Diane works her way into her two new roles, Blaine supports her all the way. But he's also interested in more than the baby. He's seriously interested in Diane. There are lots of reasons to avoid a romantic relationship, but in the end he can't.

He has to hope Diane won't wind up seeing him as an added complication in her already complicated life.

Happy reading,

Rachel Lee

A Bachelor,
a Boss and a Baby

Rachel Lee

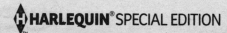
HARLEQUIN® SPECIAL EDITION

Recycling programs
for this product may
not exist in your area.

ISBN-13: 978-1-335-46574-0

A Bachelor, a Boss and a Baby

This edition published by arrangement with Harlequin Books S.A.

For questions and comments about the quality of this book, please contact us at CustomerService@Harlequin.com.

Printed in U.S.A.

Rachel Lee was hooked on writing by the age of twelve and practiced her craft as she moved from place to place all over the United States. This *New York Times* bestselling author now resides in Florida and has the joy of writing full-time.

Books by Rachel Lee

Harlequin Special Edition

Conard County: The Next Generation

A Soldier in Conard County
A Conard County Courtship
A Conard County Homecoming
His Pregnant Courthouse Bride
An Unlikely Daddy
A Cowboy for Christmas
The Lawman Lassoes a Family
A Conard County Baby
Reuniting with the Rancher
Thanksgiving Daddy
The Widow of Conard County

Montana Mavericks: 20 Years in the Saddle!

A Very Maverick Christmas

Harlequin Intrigue

Conard County: The Next Generation

Cornered in Conard County

Harlequin Romantic Suspense

Conard County: The Next Generation

Undercover in Conard County
Conard County Marine
A Conard County Spy
A Secret in Conard County
Conard County Witness

Visit the Author Profile page
at Harlequin.com for more titles.

Chapter One

Blaine Harrigan might have been the most delighted man in all of Conard County when he heard that a new planning manager had been hired. For years now the position had been vacant, the comprehensive plan was at least ten years old and he'd been dealing with all the county engineering while aware that they needed to update the plan. And he needed someone between him and the planning boards, which were made up of city council and county commission members. A little conflict of interest didn't make his job any easier, especially with an out-of-date plan that they overrode readily *because* it was so old.

When he heard they'd hired Diane Finch, he'd read over her résumé and given a huge sigh of relief. She looked competent and had great recommendations from her previous job in Des Moines. Better, she sounded more than capable of standing up with him to the so-called planning boards that had started looking more to their personal interests than what was best for the county and city.

Well, maybe she wouldn't stand up with him at first, not with her job so new, and not until she learned the lay of the land. But a professional planner? She probably wouldn't be keen to play along with ideas that could make her look bad or adversely affect her career.

What's more, she had to be aware that the county and city couldn't get useful grants without an updated plan and a planner to write the proposals and oversee performance.

He'd probably have to wait awhile for the ally to emerge regardless. That was all right with him. He'd been poking his finger into the dike to stop the rash of self-serving plans for over five years now.

More than once he'd considered looking for another job, but his Irish blood wouldn't let him run from a fight. Besides, he'd grown fond of Conard County, different in so many ways from Galway, where he'd grown up. Life had brought him here, and while he'd always be homesick for the beauties of Galway, he found different beauty here in the mountains and rolling prairie. He'd also found a place he was willing to defend and maybe sink some permanent roots.

With that random assortment of thoughts rolling

around in his head, he strolled through the basement hallways in the courthouse, heading to the rooms that belonged to the planner. Diane Finch, according to the grapevine, had arrived early this morning, and for some reason the court clerks and the many city and county employees who filled the offices down here had been looking rather amused and whispering quite a bit.

He wanted to know what was going on. Was she a golden-scaled dragon or something?

Painting a smile on his face, he knocked briefly on the closed door and entered, ready to meet the woman he hoped would work with him. The sound that came through the door should have warned him, but since it shouldn't be there, he'd assumed it was drifting down from the floor above.

He froze in astonishment as he stepped in. The unlikeliest of sights greeted him.

A lovely young woman with golden-blond hair, wearing what appeared to be a gray slacks suit, stood at a bare desk with a baby on it. She appeared to be busy trying to put a fresh diaper on the squalling, struggling bundle of pink bottom and pulled-up yellow cloth. The golden eyes that rose in surprise to look at him also appeared almost frantic.

Questions could come later, he decided in an instant. Swiftly closing the door behind him, he asked, "Need a little help there?" His brogue, so carefully erased, somehow pushed its way through.

"You've got kids?" she asked almost plaintively.

"I helped raise me five brothers and sisters. You're new at this?"

"Very," she admitted.

Without any hesitation, he rounded her desk and nudged her aside a bit. "I'm used to cloth diapers," he remarked, holding the baby safely with a big hand placed gently on her tummy. The little bottom didn't look irritated, so he just went about grabbing a wipe from an open container beside a disposable diaper at the corner of the desk. He cleaned the tot quickly before opening the fresh diaper with one hand and placing it on the little girl. Despite the child's wildly waving arms and legs, it only took a few seconds, then he had her diapered and dry. Pulling down her onesie, he fastened the snaps easily.

Instead of quieting, the baby continued to cry.

"She been fed?" he asked.

"Just."

"Ah." Without another word he picked the child up and placed her on his shoulder, not caring he was probably going to need a fresh shirt after this. "Hush, little treasure," he murmured, gently patting and rubbing her back with practiced ease while pacing the small office. After he took about a dozen steps back and forth, the babe's fist found its way to her mouth and she quieted. Moments after that a small burp escaped her.

"There we go," Blaine said, "but it's probably not the last. You mind?"

She sank into the chair behind the desk and gave

him a crooked smile. "Not at all. I'm so totally new to this I'm learning everything the hard way."

"No prior practice, then?"

She shook her head. "Daphne is my cousin's child. She's in the hospital and I'm fostering. I thought it would be easy."

Blaine allowed a quiet chuckle to escape him. "It's not hard. You probably need to worry a whole lot less. Unless the tot is sick, what it most needs is love, food and a clean nappy. Simple. And it will all go a lot easier when you relax."

She looked askance.

"She feels your nervousness, so she gets uneasy. By the way, I take it you're Diane Finch?"

She nodded. "And you're…?"

"County engineer. Blaine Harrigan. Do the bosses know you've got company?"

"You mean Daphne? No. I was hoping I could find decent day care when I arrived in town. That *certainly* isn't as easy as I thought. I'm also learning I have a lot of qualms about leaving her with someone I don't know." She sighed and drummed her fingers briefly on the arms of her chair. "This is going to cost me my job, isn't it?"

"Bringing the baby to work? I suppose it could. I also suppose I could help you batter the bosses down. It's only temporary, after all."

She sighed and closed her eyes. "That's a nice offer, Mr. Harrigan, but I'm very much afraid this isn't going to be temporary. At least not the part where I foster Daphne. I should get some kind of day care sorted out, though."

"Then we'll start with that," he said. Now he had a sleeping child on his shoulder and he was reluctant to put her down in the car seat in the corner. He also wanted to know what had happened to bring Diane Finch to the point of taking care of her cousin's baby indefinitely when she was obviously so unprepared for the task.

She was a beautiful woman, all right. He couldn't help but notice the way that satiny blouse caressed her breasts when she moved and her jacket fell open. Nice shape, adorable face and what appeared to be natural blond hair. Attractive like a flower to a bee. *Not the time to be thinking such things, boyo*, he told himself.

But now he was also seriously intrigued. "So, how did you come to be a foster mother?"

Her face closed a bit. "My cousin is seriously ill. She can't care for Daphne and probably won't be able to for a long time. That left me or putting her in the foster care system. Maybe for adoption, although my cousin…" She broke off. "Anyway, it's me and Daphne for as long as she needs me."

That raised more questions than it answered, but he let it go. She didn't know him from Adam, and this was very personal ground. There were few secrets in Conard County because most people knew each other, but Diane was new and she was probably going to face a lot of prying. He well remembered how he'd been questioned. A new face always drew attention. He didn't need to add to it.

But he had to admit to feeling some admiration for a woman who'd foster her cousin's baby while starting a new job. Not many would want the combination, he was certain. And Diane, by all appearances, was very new to this baby thing. He wondered if she'd find it presumptuous if he offered to help. Probably. Talk about sticking his nose in the tent.

Bemused, Diane watched the tall, muscular man holding tiny Daphne on his shoulder with such ease and calm. Daphne had come to her care only four days ago, when she'd been almost packed and ready to hit the road. Her cousin MaryJo, with whom she'd never been very close, had been committed indefinitely to a mental hospital with paranoid schizophrenia. Diane had been too busy the last couple of weeks to do more than to peek in on MaryJo and her new baby, and hear how sick she had become. The three-month-old Daphne had barely entered her consciousness until the social worker had told her that Daphne would have to go into long-term foster care because MaryJo couldn't possibly be a safe caretaker.

The instant she heard the words *foster care*, Daphne had loomed large on her radar, far larger than her poor cousin. Diane simply could not let that darling baby go to strangers, and the social worker also pointed out that MaryJo was too mentally ill to legally put the child up for adoption.

Adoption?

There wasn't even a father to turn to. Whoever he'd been, he was apparently long gone.

Adoption? No.

The last days had turned into a whirlwind of packing, signing papers, gaining permission to take the child to her new job, getting baby supplies and a travel bed—oh, yeah, and a car seat—then Daphne had been delivered into her care.

Diane had never doubted that this was right thing to do, but it had all landed on her like a train wreck, and she was still figuring out how to handle everything. Most especially how to care for the baby. She didn't have siblings, and she'd never watched anyone else's kids because she'd been too busy with an after-school job at a local law office. What did she know about kids?

Only that she couldn't let Daphne wind up in the foster care system. And part of her problem, as she'd discovered since she'd arrived in town two days ago, was that she didn't want to leave the baby in anyone else's hands, either. Most day care around here was in-home. The one early-learning center didn't have an opening. Her reluctance to trust someone else with the baby's care was likely to become a big issue.

So here she was, her first day on the job, with a baby. Yeah, she expected trouble, but she didn't know what else to do. She couldn't have begun to explain why she cared so much about a baby she'd only had for a few days, or why she was feeling so reluctant to put her in a stranger's care while she worked.

Yet a stranger had just diapered Daphne with practiced ease and was now pacing slowly with the sleeping girl on his shoulder. Daphne was still tiny at three months, but Blaine Harrigan made her look minuscule.

He was dressed casually in a short-sleeved khaki work shirt and jeans. The last place she had worked, a polo shirt and slacks was as informal as it got. Apparently things were different here. He certainly looked like a man ready to work hard, a sharp contrast to the way he handled Daphne: easily, gently, yet confidently. She envied that confidence. She wished she could siphon off a gallon of it and put it in her veins.

Well, she'd get there eventually. She'd learned everything else she'd needed to in life. Usually. God, she hoped she wasn't kidding herself and running headlong into a big failure.

"Are you looking forward to this job?" he asked her.

For the first time, she realized that his voice seemed to resonate from deep within his chest, below baritone but maybe not quite bass? An interesting, slightly rough sound. "I think so, yes. I know I was before life got out of hand."

He smiled faintly. "This little one, you mean? Ah, she won't be any trouble now. I was wondering, you worked in a larger city before. Why come to a small town?"

"The challenge," she said. "An outdated comprehensive plan that needs to be rewritten, and that covers an entire county. I'll have a lot of input. I've always wanted that."

He hesitated as if he wanted to say something, but then resumed his gentle pacing, rubbing Daphne's back all the while. "Did you visit first?"

"Of course. I came out for the interview. I'm surprised I didn't meet you then." And she was. They'd have to work closely together. She began to wonder how this place functioned.

"I was on vacation. I didn't hear a thing about you until I got back."

Okay, that was strange, she thought. Given his position, he should have had some say in her hiring. For the first time, she felt uneasiness about the job itself. Was there something going on here? But she couldn't ask Harrigan, because he worked here, too. Until she had a read on everyone involved, asking questions could be dangerous. Wisdom dictated that she keep everything on a professional level.

Although that was already a limit she had broken, considering her infant cousin was riding on the shoulder of the county engineer. Very professional. Under other circumstances, she might have been amused. Starting a new job, not so much.

Then, for the first time, she really saw his face. Looked at it and took it in, and felt her stomach flutter. Dark, nearly black hair with blue eyes so bright the color was arresting. The rest of that face was great, too, squarish, a good chin, with fair, unblemished skin. His last name suggested he was Irish, as did a few hints in his pronunciation. He couldn't have left the isle very long ago, she thought. Western sun and wind hadn't kissed him for long.

Fortunately, Daphne made a small sound, drawing Diane's attention before she stared at Blaine too long. Somebody should have warned her that a man holding an infant was more irresistible than one standing solo. She never would have dreamed. She watched as he pulled a visitor's chair back from her desk and slowly lowered himself into it. The chair was springy, and he rocked gently.

Then she felt embarrassed. "Would you like me to take her back?"

He smiled over the baby's head. "It's been a while since I held a baby. I'm liking it."

She felt her mouth frame a smile in return. She had to admit that this early into her new role as a mother, she was glad of a brief break. She'd had no idea that her patience wasn't infinite, that she'd be losing a lot of sleep and that she could get frazzled by a baby's persistent crying.

The new character insights didn't exactly make her feel proud. Now she not only needed to deal with a job and the baby, but she needed to deal with herself, as well.

"So what brought you here, Blaine? I'm assuming you didn't grow up here." An assumption based on those faint traces of an accent.

"No, I grew up in Ireland, I did. Galway. I'm liking it quite a bit here, but missing my family."

"You said a big family?"

"I'm one of six. The eldest."

"That's a big family," she agreed.

He leaned back a little farther and crossed his legs loosely. Tight denim left no doubt that his lower half was built as well as his top half. Diane swallowed and dragged her gaze away.

After a bit, he spoke again. "You look tired. Not sleeping well?"

Finally she felt a bubble of real amusement, for the first time in days. She'd begun to wonder if she still had a sense of humor. "What do *you* think?" An attempted joke that might have sounded like a challenge, but his demeanor didn't change. God, was she going to have to watch her tongue now, as well? Somehow she needed to get more sleep.

He nodded. "Babies are hard at first. It does get better, though. Just snatch your sleep whenever you can. So has anyone primed you for how things run around here?"

She sat up a little, fatigue forgotten. "What do I need to know?"

"Only that members of the city council and the county commission make up the county planning board. Two hats, you might say."

She wanted to drop her head into her hands. In an

instant she began to envision a skein of tangled relationships all knotted up with ego and personal aims.
No real control on them at all, except for when they
might get angry at one another. Why had they even
wanted a planning manager?

Oh, yeah. They needed an updated comprehensive plan in order to apply for government grants.
She was the path to get there. To be fair, however, her
job always became political at some point. Money
carried a lot of weight, and developers had enough
of it to be persuasive.

She had hoped, however, that she might be little
less boxed in here. Small population, for one thing,
and no rapid growth for a while. Most of what was
needed was bringing the plan up-to-date on new regulations from the state and federal government. Environmental regulations had increased dramatically...
and there was seldom a way around them. She had
that on her side, at least. Also, she needed to create a
plan that would display a good future for the county
and city, a good environment for the people as well
as one that encouraged careful growth.

Still, it was bound to be tough, and even tougher
when the cabal running matters was very small.

She kept her face smooth, however. She didn't
know Blaine Harrigan and didn't dare express anything untoward. Now that she was here with her
cousin's baby in her care, she couldn't afford to lose
her job. To protect herself, she had to stay here at
least a year, so she wouldn't put a problem smack at

the top of her résumé. Wonderful. She couldn't afford a catastrophe.

"You get used to it," he rumbled, gently patting Daphne's back. "When are you supposed to meet with the gentlemen and lady?"

"Tomorrow evening. I hope by then I can find childcare. Do you know of anyone good?" she asked hopefully. If she had to choose someone, she'd rather they came with a recommendation.

A quiet laugh escaped him. The baby stirred a little and settled quickly. "I'm not in the way of having a family. But I have friends I can ask. I'll call around today." He rose slowly, taking care not to jar the baby. "I need to be off. I've got a meeting at ten a few miles out of town about a road repair. Might require some work on the culvert. I'd invite you but for the wee bit, here."

"Oh." A truncated pointless response, but she was holding her breath anyway as he slowly bent and placed Daphne in her car seat. To her relief, the child didn't wake.

"I'll see you later," Blaine said as he straightened. He winked at her. "We'll be together a lot. In fact, you and me might need to become a damn army of two." A nod, then he let himself out.

An army of two? Diane bit her lip wondering what he meant. Had it been some kind of warning? Then she wondered at the ease with which he'd taken over with Daphne. Too bad he wasn't looking for childcare work.

Resting her chin on her hand, she looked down at the baby and wondered how all this had happened. Well, the job, at least, was her fault. It might turn out to be a very good job, too, despite what she'd heard from Blaine.

But Daphne? While she was having trouble facing it herself, it remained that Daphne's presence in her life was probably going to be long term. As in permanent.

MaryJo had been growing sicker for years, but it had been a slow process. A lot of it had been brushed away as quirks. Then, last year, MaryJo's parents had died in a flash flood in Texas, and that seemed to have pushed MaryJo past her tipping point.

First had come the social workers, then had come a pregnancy during which she couldn't take any meds, and the next thing Diane had known, her cousin had a full-blown psychotic break. After the baby was born, the meds didn't help much.

MaryJo heard voices that told her to do terrible things. She even hallucinated. In short, MaryJo had vanished into an alternate universe, and nobody believed it was safe to leave Daphne in her care, or even nearby. To this day, Diane was ashamed of how little time she'd spared for thinking of her cousin on the far side of the state. She'd gotten the wrap-up from a social worker after MaryJo was hospitalized.

Then, a little less than three months after Daphne's birth, the baby had come to live with Diane.

Inevitably, though, Diane looked down at the

sleeping child and smiled. Except when Daphne was fussing and inconsolable, Diane always felt happy looking at her. Something about a baby.

Then she turned back to her desk and opened the folder containing all the notes for her new job that someone had left.

Around noon, a quiet knock sounded on her office door. She glanced at the still sleeping Daphne and decided she'd better answer it rather than call out. Rising, she rounded her desk and opened the door to find two women of about her own age, early thirties, standing there with big smiles. One had silky chestnut hair to her shoulders and wore a Western shirt with a denim skirt and cowboy boots. The other was a redhead who wore a flaming red slacks suit that she carried off with panache.

"I'm Aubrey," said chestnut hair. "And this is my friend Candy. We're in the clerk's office. We heard you brought your baby, and everybody is dying to see her, so we thought we'd skip down here first and prepare you. And maybe you'd like to go to lunch with us?"

At once startled and charmed, Diane returned the smile. "You can peek, ladies, but she's sleeping for the first time since 1:00 a.m. I'd rather nothing wake her."

"Of course not," said Aubrey, keeping her voice low. "I've been through it. Sleep before everything."

Deciding it was okay, Diane stepped back and

opened the door wider. Both women crept in quietly and looked down on the angelic baby who only a few hours ago had been wearing horns and carrying a pitchfork. The mental image suddenly made Diane want to laugh.

"Ooh, how sweet," breathed Candy. "She's so pretty. And that's saying something about such a young one."

Aubrey elbowed her gently. "Wait till you have your own. But yeah, she's gorgeous, all right. We'll tell everyone to give you space, but now we can report back so they won't be so curious. I didn't know you were bringing a family. I thought you were single. Well, we all did."

Diane flushed, realizing that the questioning had begun. She wondered how long before it turned into a cross examination.

"I am single. This is my cousin's baby. I'm taking care of her because my cousin is seriously ill."

"That's a shame," said Aubrey. "About your cousin, I mean. Well, I guess you don't want to carry the baby across the way to the diner, but would you like us to bring you back lunch? And if you like coffee, don't get it out of the machine in the hallway. It's terrible. But walk half a block and you'll get it world-class."

"That's good to know, because I do love coffee and tea. Especially a latte, but…"

"Oh, we're part of the modern world," said Candy. "The diner makes lattes. I do wish we'd get a decent Chinese or Mexican restaurant, though. Maude's great, but basic." She hesitated, then asked, "Do you want a salad or a sandwich? I can recommend the Cobb salad."

"Or the steak sandwich," Aubrey chimed in quietly. "That usually makes two meals for me. You wouldn't have to cook tonight."

"I love Cobb salads," Diane said, but she couldn't help thinking about a steak sandwich. Full of calories, but over two meals… "Let me get my purse. I think I'll have the sandwich, after all."

Candy quickly waved her hand. "Consider this a welcome-to-town present. It's just a little thing. While we're out, does the baby need anything?"

Yesterday's trip to the market had pretty much taken care of that. "I'm stocked," she said with confidence.

The women both smiled and began to make their quiet way to the door. Then Aubrey looked back. "Do you need day care?"

Diane's heart leaped. "Yes. But…"

"You don't know who to trust," Aubrey finished. "How could you, being new in town? My brother's wife works at the early-learning center. I'll see if she can find you a space. Be back in a short while?"

With waves, the women left. Diane checked on the baby once again then settled at her desk, wishing for coffee and an answer to cosmic questions. She'd been so career focused until this, but now she had another life to worry about.

Forgetting the folder she needed to read, she sat and stared at the nearby baby. Daphne had already changed everything, and Diane suspected the changes had only just begun.

She just wished she had some experience to guide her.

Blaine stood on the road in question, surveying the situation. The road was elevated a few feet above the surrounding ranch land, which helped keep it dry and, in the case of blowing snow, relatively snow-free much of the winter.

But there was no question that the recent heavy rain and runoff had caused the road to dip dangerously, right over a culvert meant to equalize water buildup between the grazing land on either side and to prevent ponding as much as possible. But the recent rains had been anything but usual for this area, and problems had begun to turn up.

Climbing down to a lower position, Blaine scanned the figures the surveyor had gathered, then eyed the situation for himself. The question was whether they could save the culvert and road simply by clearing the asphalt, building up a layer of solid earth and gravel, then repaving over it.

Neither option would be cheap for the penny-pinching county commission, but the right option had to be chosen regardless of cost. A road cave-in could cause worse problems. And no matter what his decision, a lot of people were going to be bothered by a necessary detour.

His colleague Doug Ashbur, from the roads department, was inspecting the other end of the culvert. He called along it to Blaine the instant he saw him.

"Abandon hope," Doug called, his voice echoing. "I don't know about your end, but the metal's rusting out down here, and the concrete casement is cracking."

"Grand." The view from his end wasn't any better. He saw more than rusting steel and cracking concrete. He also saw a definite dip in culvert beneath the sinking road. The entire thing was trying to collapse.

He stepped back a few yards, being wiser than to enter that culvert in its current condition. Past engineers and road builders had tried their best, but the simple fact was that with the typical hypercold winter temperatures and the eventual thaws, that concrete was bound to crack. Even a minuscule crack would worsen with temperature changes, the ice expanding when water filled the small cracks, enlarging them, until this. The galvanized steel pipe under the concrete had been someone's attempt years ago to prevent a catastrophic failure.

It had worked so far, but now it was a question of how long they had.

He eyed the ground above the culvert, beneath the road, and saw evidence that the ground was extruding from the smooth slope that must have once been there. So the concrete was no longer adequately bearing the weight of the road, the steel pipe was collapsing and the ground between the culvert and road had evidently washed away from the weeks of rain that must have penetrated through cracks in the old asphalt. An accident waiting to happen.

He called to Doug. "We'd better redirect traffic and close this road. See you up top." He climbed the bank, using his hands when necessary, then went to his truck, where he pulled off his thick leather work gloves and stood staring at the dip.

It didn't look like much now. There was also no way to be sure when it would become a big deal. It was far too weakened to be driving trucks and cars over, but it might last months. Even through the winter. And that was counting on luck a bit too much for his taste.

Up here he could feel the ceaseless breeze that never stopped in open places. While it was early autumn, the air was still warm and smelled a bit like summer. A very different summer than in Galway: warmer, drier, dustier. Sometimes he missed the cooler, wetter clime of home, but mostly he liked it here. Different, but with its own beauty, like when he turned to look at the mountains that loomed so close to the west. Any morning now he'd wake up to see the sugary coating of a first snowfall.

Doug joined him. "I'll order up equipment, Blaine. It might be a few days before I can get it all together. You know how it goes."

He most certainly did. This county didn't have any resources to waste, and his too many bosses all had their eyes on things beyond the event horizon, like finally getting that oft-promised ski resort built and finding other ways to make this county more attractive and create jobs. Oh, and wealth. He was sure that had to fit in somewhere.

The ranchers around here weren't much interested in the big schemes. They just wanted to survive another year. But that meant they needed decent enough roads to carry cattle to the stockyard at the train station, roads over which to get to town and see their kids get to school…oh, a million reasons why folks these days couldn't just be cut off from the rest of the world for months at a time.

Like it or not, expensive or not, the county was going to have to fix this culvert.

"I believe we've got enough in the budget," he said to Doug. "This clearly can't wait."

"I agree. But we've got a dozen others that aren't much better."

"At least they're not already collapsing. Let's get the signs up. You have some barricades?"

Doug laughed. "Never travel without them. Okay, I'll work on pulling together the equipment and crew." He paused, looking back at the dip in the road. "How you want to do this? Another culvert?"

"We talked about other solutions, you remember. The problem is that if we don't use culverts, the erosion just expands to eat the road." As dry as this place was in general, he was often surprised how much of a headache water gave him. Usually in the spring, however. The last rains had been record-breaking for September.

While he put out some orange cones and staked some detour signs at the crossroad, his thoughts wandered back to Diane. He wondered how she was going to like dealing with the good ol' boys of Conard County. He wondered if they'd give her a hard time about the baby.

Mostly he wondered why she was haunting his thoughts and why he kept thinking she was a tidy armful. And why his body stirred in response.

Well, he assured himself, that would wear off. It had to. Anyway, he'd hardly talked to her. Chances were he wouldn't continue to feel the sexual draw when he learned what she was really like.

Wasn't that always the way?

Chapter Two

Diane went to her little rented house that night with a briefcase full of files that had been left on her desk and a baby who'd eaten enough today to satisfy a horse…well, relatively speaking. It seemed as if she needed to be fed about every two or three hours, even though the social worker had said that should begin to slow down. Not yet, obviously, and it might continue through the night.

Oh, yeah, get the girl a pediatrician. Maybe she ought to start keeping a list so she didn't forget something. The move and taking charge of an infant had left her a bit scatterbrained.

At the last moment, before settling into a small house she hadn't yet been able to turn into a home, she thought to check her diaper stash even though she'd bought quite a few yesterday. Who would have thought such a bitty thing could fill so many diapers?

She counted and decided she had enough for a couple of days. Plenty of formula, too. And since Candy and Aubrey had brought her a huge lunch from the café, she didn't need to cook.

Good heavens, she thought. The baby was sleeping contentedly, she could dine without cooking and she had time to kick off her shoes and collapse on the recliner that had been delivered just yesterday. Beaten and creaky, it held a lot of memories of her father, a veteran who had largely retreated to a distant land inside his own head. Memories of her father, as rare as the good ones had been, were something she didn't want to lose entirely.

She wandered down the hall to the bedroom she hadn't had time to unpack yet and opened a suitcase to pull out her favorite old jeans and a checked shirt as softened by age as the jeans. Her grungies, her comfies, whatever anyone wanted to call them. That night she had nothing to do except care for Daphne and herself...for the first time since she'd accepted this job. She supposed she ought to feel slothful for not unpacking just a little, but frankly, she was worn out. She could live out of a suitcase for another day.

When she emerged from her bedroom, slightly freshened for the evening, she heard Daphne stirring, making little sounds that might soon turn into a full-throated cry. Diaper. Feeding. Blaine had been right about one thing: it was actually very simple. Demanding but simple.

In a very short time, she had become practiced at pulling out a bottle and filling it with room-temperature formula from a can. The woman who had turned Daphne over to Diane had told her she didn't need to warm the baby bottles as long as the formula was at room temperature. However, it had been chilly outside, so she put the bottle in a pan of warm water from the sink and gave it a few minutes to lose any chill.

She tested the warmth of the formula on the inside of her wrist, then went to rescue her increasingly noisy charge. A finger in the diaper told her that could wait, so she gathered the child to her and let her drink from the bottle.

Sitting in her recliner without putting her feet up, she became fascinated with watching Daphne eat. Her little eyes, beginning to get darker and resemble her mother's, watched her back. Intense. Content.

Amazing. After just a few days she could feel her heart reaching out to this child, taking her in, wrapping her in swiftly growing love. If MaryJo got well, it was going to hurt to have to give this baby up. Hurt like hell.

But the social worker's assessment had been brutal: MaryJo would never be well enough to care for her own child. If she improved, like so many with her illness, she probably couldn't be trusted to stay on her meds. And if she didn't keep taking her medication…

Diane shook her head a little and began to hum softly. Daphne continued to watch her, then with a surprisingly strong thrust of arms and legs, she turned her head from the bottle.

"Enough of that, huh?" Diane asked. "A little gas bubble, maybe? You eat more than that."

Daphne scrunched up her face, so Diane quickly put the girl over her shoulder and began to pat and rub her back. She felt a bit embarrassed that Blaine had done it for her earlier, clearly thinking she didn't know to do such a thing. But she'd forgotten in the midst of her overwhelming day.

She wouldn't forget now. Rising from the chair, she paced and patted, continuing to hum quietly. When the little burp emerged, she offered more formula.

"Easy peasy," Diane said. Twenty minutes later, she had the child changed—she decided she was going to need a changing table soon—dressed in a fresh onesie and apparently content enough to yawn.

"Success." The best evening yet. She paced with the little girl on her shoulder some more, drawing out another tiny burp, then moved her to the cradle of her arm. Daphne waved one fist around then shoved it toward her mouth. In an eye blink, she fell asleep.

A very successful evening. Diane was smiling happily as she settled Daphne into her small travel bed. She needed to get a crib soon, too. But first there'd be another round of hungry baby around eleven.

One of her girlfriends had told her before she left her old job that she was lucky, missing the first three months of caring for the baby. "By four months," Lucy had said, "I was beginning to wonder if the little brat would ever sleep through the night. You remember. I was in a fog of sleep deprivation all the time."

Diane didn't really remember, because she hadn't seen a whole lot of Lucy after she birthed her first child. "Too busy" had been Lucy's response to every invitation. She probably had been, too.

For that matter, she felt a bit guilty about how little she'd seen of MaryJo in the past five years. The kind of closeness some claimed with cousins had never existed between them, and there was little enough to pull them together when they no longer lived in the same town.

MaryJo's parents had divorced a long time ago. She'd never seen her dad again. Then her mother had dived into a bottle and never emerged. The most amazing thing was that those two had been together when they got caught in a flash flood in Texas. As if they might have been reaching out to one another again? No one would ever know now.

It was hardly to be wondered that MaryJo was troubled, but the social worker assured her that the causes of schizophrenia involved so many factors nobody could pin all of them down. Bottom line, she really didn't need to worry about Daphne getting it.

Diane hoped that was so. She couldn't imagine that darling child growing up to be so ill.

She was just about to move to the recliner and close her eyes for a little while before heating up the remains of her lunch when someone knocked at the door.

Her heart accelerated. She'd come from a much larger city where knocks on the door at this time of night were a bit threatening. Too late for regular deliveries, and friends always called first. Plus, she really didn't know anyone here, so it couldn't possibly be a friendly call, could it?

On the other hand, as an official now, her address was had become public record, so finding her wouldn't be hard if someone wanted to rant about something. Lovely idea.

But she shook herself, telling herself not to be ridiculous, and went to answer it.

She should have guessed. Blaine Harrigan stood there, wearing a light jacket now and holding a potted red gerbera daisy. "To brighten a windowsill," he said with a smile. "I take it your new boss is happily sleeping?"

Just seeing him drew a bright smile from her and a rush of warmth. Man, she didn't even know this guy. It was too soon to be happy to see him, wasn't it?

Heck, she didn't care. It was nice to see him, to feel as if she might have made her first friend here.

She stepped back, inviting him in. "Thank you for the daisy. I just love it. What a kind thought." She looked at the bright flower with a sudden feeling of comfort, as if she weren't a total stranger here anymore. "I was thinking about making some tea. Would you like some?"

"I never turn down a cuppa," he answered. He handed her the flower, and she motioned him to follow her to the small kitchen and dining area. She placed the daisy on the sill over the sink then turned to find him standing in the doorway, evidently awaiting an invitation to sit or go.

"Have a seat," she said, pointing to the ridiculously small table with two chairs. This place had come partially furnished, a relief to her because she hadn't wanted to ship her things from Iowa. None of it had been worth shipping. Her life revolved around her work, and decorating had mostly involved plastic storage containers and repurposed boxes. Hey, it had served her needs.

But now…well, what was here could do with a few additions for the baby.

"So you're enjoying a little peace and quiet," he said as she filled the kettle and put it on the gas stove.

"Until around eleven," she agreed. "I'm sorry you caught me in such a mess earlier. I'm new at this, but I'm not stupid. I don't know why I didn't think of burping Daphne. I do it all the time!"

He laughed quietly. "No excuses needed. You're tired, probably overwhelmed. I mean, a new job and a new baby all at once? And more to come, I believe. I'll bet the little one starts creeping and crawling soon."

"She's already trying," Diane admitted. "When I put her down on a blanket. But I've only had four days with her. A lot to learn." She hesitated. "You said you were from Ireland, right?"

He nodded.

"Then my tea is probably going to appall you."

He leaned forward a little on his chair. "Tea bags? I've learned to admire their advantages. Easy and quick, especially for a single guy who only wants one cup. Now, if I really want to brew a pot, I can do it, but usually I'm on the run."

"I wouldn't even know where to begin. I make a pot with tea bags."

"I'll show you when we have some time. Anyway, I'm going to buzz into yer meetin' with the commissioners tomorrow."

"The culvert?" she asked, turning to pull out two mugs and a box of tea bags and put them on the table.

"It has to be replaced quickly. The road is sinking, the concrete is cracking and the steel drainage pipe is buckling. Me and Doug from the road department closed off the road today. I don't want some poor rancher to start driving over it and find his bonnet—sorry, hood—six feet in the ground."

Diane nodded. "Not good. Do you like milk and sugar?"

"I'll go for straight. Thanks. Yeah, the budget has

been way too tight for too long. Been patching and mending as best we can, but there's only so long we can push things off."

"I know. Infrastructure is one of my pet peeves. Nothing works if you haven't got it."

"Ah, some common sense!"

She couldn't repress a giggle at that. She wasn't totally unfamiliar with the difficulties he mentioned. No place ran like a smoothly oiled machine, no budget was ever sufficient and personalities always got in the way. "Did you expect something else from an urban planner?"

His grin broadened. "I've known all types in my life."

She was still smiling as she poured boiling water into the mugs over the waiting tea bags. Soon the rich aroma of black tea began to waft through the kitchen. "So why did you leave Ireland?" she asked. "I've always wanted to go there."

"Now that's a story," he answered. Once again his deep voice took on the rhythms of the American West, leaving behind the hints of Galway. And they were just hints, poking out from time to time. He'd clearly been in the States for a while. "Like many places in the world, Ireland was booming just before the economic crash. Unlike many places in the world, we didn't recover quickly. We had too much boom. We were bringing in workers from all over the world, building fast, growing, and then..." He shrugged.

"Whatever. Life was getting harder, finding work

was getting harder and I had a bit of the wanderlust in me. I hopped through a few jobs, then stopped here."

"Why?"

He shrugged. "Because I like it. It's different. Galway's beautiful with mountains and plenty of seashore, and the town itself has a lot of charm in parts. But I have to say, I wasn't prepared for the sheer size of your country. I was astonished and spellbound. And then I saw the mountains here. They dwarf anything I'd ever known before, plus there's a whole lot of wide-open space, space almost beyond imagining. It would be hard to tear me away."

She nodded and set her tea bag on the saucer in the middle of the table. Lifting her cup, she closed her eyes for a few seconds just to inhale the fragrant steam. The questions buzzing her head were dangerous, so she diverted. She didn't dare ask about people she would be working with. "All tea comes from a single Asian plant, from Yunnan in China. It grows elsewhere now, and there are probably varieties, but most of the flavor we love has to do with how the tea is aged." She opened her eyes.

"Where did that come from?" he asked.

"Trying to avoid asking you about the members of the commissions and boards I'm going to be dealing with."

He cracked a laugh, a deep sound that rumbled as if it rose from the depths. "I shouldn't say much. A bunch of eejits, but not always. They're politicians.

You can count on them to look out for themselves. Take the culvert I told you about. That's going to need to be replaced as swiftly as possible. I'll have to let them know what I'm going to do, even though I believe I have the money in the roads budget. They like to be informed. Oh, keep that in mind, Diane. They want to know everything. Some of them will raise Cain because there are probably ten things that they might consider more important. Finally they'll settle down and give me the go-ahead simply because they don't want a dozen of the largest ranchers around here to be having to detour by miles all winter. But the argument will reassure them that they're the ones in control."

She understood him perfectly. That was a game she'd played before. She also knew how to win… usually.

"But that's just a handful of people," he said. "The rest of the folks around here are the kind of people I'm happy to spend time with. At least those I've met. I think you'll enjoy most everything here, unless you like to live in high style. The closest thing we have to a nightclub is a roadhouse, where I'd advise you to never go alone. Then there's Mahoney's Bar, which is as close as I've ever found to my local pub." He paused. "Now, you might like that somewhat. Busy, friendly place."

She was smiling again, enjoying his description. Relaxation had begun to fill her anew as she thought that she probably hadn't made a mistake in accepting this job.

Daphne's sudden entrance into her life had given Diane more qualms about coming to Conard County than she'd initially had by far. When it was just her, it was all a big adventure. With Daphne it had become intimidating. She had begun to start thinking about all kinds of things, from day care to eventual schooling. Was this the best place to give her little cousin all the opportunities she should have? And what about the quality of medical care?

Thoughts that had never plagued her before plagued her now. "Becoming an unexpected mother is a bit shocking," she said, musing and only half-aware she was speaking. "A whole new set of worries I never had in the past, and bam, at the worst time possible, in the middle of a move and starting a new job."

"Yeah, most people get a little more warning, like about nine months."

Again he made her laugh. There was a sparkle in his amazing blue eyes and only humor around his mouth. A good-looking man. She realized she was experiencing an adolescent urge to just drink him in with her eyes. At once she raised her cup and turned her attention to her tea, hoping to find safety there. She had too much on her plate, and anyway, as far as she could determine, romantic relationships with colleagues could be fraught with danger and a lot of potential discomfort.

"Thanks so much for the tea," he said, rising. He crossed to the sink and rinsed his cup before setting it on the counter. "I'll see you in the morning, Diane. I'm sure you need some downtime after everything."

She rose, too, and followed him to the door. "How much trouble do you think they're going to give me over Daphne? Aubrey said she'll ask her sister-in-law to find room for her at the day care center."

He paused with his hand on the doorknob and gave her another smile. "I told you we were going to be an army. I meant it. First one gives you a hard time is going to hear from me. You're entitled to time to settle everything. Good night."

"Thank you again for the flower," she called after him.

He gave a quick wave, then strode away into the night. He moved easily, evidently fit and apparently accustomed to walking. He passed from the pool of light under one streetlamp to the next until he vanished around a corner.

Only then did she close and lock her door. Back in the kitchen, she smiled again as she looked at the bright red daisy on her windowsill. A thoughtful gesture. He couldn't possibly have guessed how much she loved gerbera daisies. They always reminded her of a drawing, so perfect it hardly seemed possible that they were real.

Then, trying to divert her thoughts from Blaine without much success, she put the remains of her steak sandwich and salad on a plate, opened a bottle of diet root beer and headed for her recliner.

Settled in comfortably, she waited for the next feeding and wondered if she could find that novel she'd been reading before her whole life had been packed into boxes and the trunk of her car. Having so little furniture of her own that was worth keeping had made the move easy and cheap. But now there were boxes stuffed into every corner, awaiting her attention. Boxes that had been labeled by the movers she had hired. She wondered how well they had done their jobs.

Well, she could wait to find out. The important thing was that she had her dad's easy chair.

And Daphne. That baby was becoming incredibly important to her.

Poor MaryJo. Diane couldn't begin to imagine the hell her cousin must be enduring. She just hoped the doctors could help.

Then she started eating, taking her time. Even cold the sandwich tasted delicious. She wiggled her toes and felt tension start to leave her legs.

Man, she had been wound up today, although she hadn't really been aware of it. For a little while when Daphne had refused to stop crying, yeah, then she'd been frantic.

But Blaine had come along, handling it all for her and assuring her it wasn't all that difficult a thing to take care of a baby. Then Aubrey and Candy and their warm welcome.

She just hoped tomorrow would go as well. With a full tummy, she put her empty plate and bottle onto the box beside her chair and allowed herself to doze. Behind her eyelids danced the memory of a man offering her a red gerbera daisy.

Chapter Three

For her first meeting with her new bosses as an employee, Diane chose a three-piece black outfit with slacks, a matching sleeveless shirt and a modified trapeze top that moved slightly when she walked but had the effect of minimizing her curves, such as they might be. Drawing attention to her gender had never yet proved to be an asset at work.

Daphne seemed to be in a sunny mood, eating her breakfast while looking around as if taking the whole world in. Tucked safely in her car seat, she waved her little arms and legs freely, causing Diane just a bit of trouble as she tried to strap the girl safely into the back seat of her car. Diane didn't mind the wiggling, however. She just wished she could share the child's happy mood. Right then she felt as if she might be going to her execution.

Aubrey and Candy had come to her office because they'd heard about Daphne. That probably meant everyone else with an interest had heard by now. What would she do if they refused to let her bring the child with her until she could find suitable care for her?

Her stomach had begun to feel like lead. The oat cereal she'd eaten felt like it wanted to stage a revolution. She paused to check the diaper bag once more, making sure she had enough for the day. And if she didn't, well, there was lunch hour and a trip to the pharmacy on Main Street or the grocery at the edge of town. She wasn't in the wilderness, for heaven's sake.

Mentally bucking herself up, she drove down streets beneath big old trees that were just beginning to brighten with autumn color. She had a designated parking space behind the courthouse, and she slid into it. After she turned off the engine, she sat for several minutes, trying to center herself.

She was startled by a gentle rapping on the window beside her. Turning her head, she saw a pleasant-looking man in a sweatshirt and jeans. She rolled her window down a crack.

"Hey," he said. "I'm Wyatt Carter, the judge around here. You're the new urban planner, aren't you? Is everything okay? You didn't move for so long, I had to wonder."

Diane felt her cheeks heat a bit. "I'm fine. New-job nerves."

He nodded. "I get that. Come on, I'll walk you in and we'll stare everyone down."

That made her smile at last. "Do I really need protection?"

He tilted his head as if thinking, then shook his head. "Actually, not at all. That's what I have a gavel for."

Which was how she came to be walking down the corridor in the courthouse basement with the judge carrying her diaper bag while she carried Daphne in her all-purpose car seat in one hand and her brief-case in the other.

Quite a start to the day, she thought as she entered her office. Wyatt—he'd already insisted she drop the formality—placed the diaper bag on her desk. "I'm just two floors up, and we're having a full day in the court. If you need anything from me, one of the clerks can bring me a message. But honestly, I think everyone down here will help you without hesitation. Have a great day and remind the council members I still own the gavel."

Well, he'd certainly helped her get over some of her nerves, she thought. Was this town a Disney cre-ation? Everyone she'd met so far had been amazingly nice. She placed Daphne in a corner out of the way after checking her diaper, then gave her a small, not too noisy rattle to use. Clutched in one little fist, it waved in every direction, then wound up pressed to the girl's mouth. Everything seemed to wind up there. She made a mental note to check around her house very carefully before putting the baby down on a blanket on the floor.

Or maybe she should get a playpen. Man, the list was adding up. Playpen, changing table, crib. Then more clothes, because her onesies would stop fitting soon.

Seated at her desk, she pulled the files out of her briefcase, feeling only one pang of guilt that she hadn't spent any time on them last night. Not that they needed intense attention. One was the comprehensive plan from so long ago, and she'd read that before applying. It read like comprehensive plans everywhere except for being outdated.

Then there was a series of folders that amounted to the local wish list, she guessed. Airport runway expansion. Updating the parks. Help to attract new business. Some funding for repairing the high school, which had apparently met with… She caught her breath. A bomb? Really? She wouldn't have expected that here. Probably some kid who'd thought he was being funny. Or brilliant.

The one that most caught her attention was a plan to widen one of the roads up into the mountains to turn it into a scenic drive that would end at an historic mining town that, of course, needed work to make it safe. But that was the kind of thing she loved—preserving historical sites, making them into attractions that would ensure their longevity.

Some of these projects would likely have to be handled by bond issues, but some could well qualify for grants from various sources. And that would be her job. That and updating the comprehensive plan to comply with new regulations.

Leaning back in her chair, listening to the quiet sounds of the rattle, which would probably elicit tears by falling on the floor soon, and listening to the baby noises Daphne was making, she closed her eyes and remembered why she had taken this job in the first place.

Conard County wasn't all built up like the other places she'd worked, most recently Des Moines. When she'd come out for the interview and looked around the area, all she could see was possibility. Of course, she couldn't make it all happen, and she wasn't sure it would be good for the community if she did, but some of it could be brought to life here. The potential, the virtually clean slate…yeah, a lot could be done here, and with those mountains so nearby, that merely expanded the things they could accomplish.

The scenic road was one great idea. She'd also read how repeated attempts to build a ski resort had fallen through, the last time because of some serious landslides.

She didn't understand why it couldn't be done. Those mountains weren't going anywhere, but they needed funding for an independent geological survey. That last failure had occurred because of record-breaking rain. Surely that could be planned around. Earthquake activity seemed to be minor. She'd suggest the survey as one of her projects.

Oh, she'd been bubbling with ideas since her interview, but she had to be careful to avoid the "new broom" effect. There was bound to be resistance to any change around here, so she'd better find her way among the people who'd be affected. Maybe a town hall or charette, a survey of what folks besides the commissioners wanted around here. Community input was essential.

She glanced over and saw that Daphne had fallen asleep, the rattle still clutched in tiny hands. Toys suitable for an infant, she thought, adding that to her growing mental list. She wondered what other unthought-of things lay around the corner.

She returned to the files, trying to organize them in a useful way for the work ahead of her. Sources for grants would be her first move, and for that she needed projects that might garner private funding. Turning to the computer on her desk, she opened a new digital file and began to transfer information. Why in the world were these files still paper, anyway? Had they been around that long?

Much as she didn't feel like working, she actually made some headway in her organization and was starting to feel fairly good about her morning when the door opened.

Looking up, she saw Blaine poking his head through a five-inch opening. "We're up. The mayor, the council chairman and the chief commissioner have decided they want to meet with you *now*."

Diane's stomach turned over, then became queasy. Anxiety because it was barely noon and the public meeting was supposed to be at six. "Now?" she said pointlessly.

"Well, I got you ten minutes. Better make sure the tot is comfy and you have a bottle. Don't panic, it's not the lion's den and I'll be there."

"I'm not panicking," she lied bravely. "What happened?"

"People talk. And some other people want to get the jump on their, um, colleagues. In short, they want the first whack and want information before the others get it."

She understood that all too well. When it came to personal power, adults could act like toddlers. "This isn't a good start," she remarked.

"Is any? I'll be back for you and Daphne in ten. Or would you rather I ask someone to watch her just for now?"

"Thanks, but I might as well put all the cards on the table right now." If it was to be a fight, she was ready for it, she believed. Planners like her weren't a dime a dozen.

Blaine walked down the hall, his thumbs hooked on his jeans pockets. This was indeed not a good start. The eejits had hired this woman while he was away and could offer no input, and now they were going to have a turf war over her?

He had to give her marks for taking the tot right into it with her. Apparently, Diane Finch like to have the air as clear as possible. Well, so did he.

But not the damn fools they were about to meet. Oh, no. The muddier the better for them.

Then he brushed aside the thoughts as unproductive. He'd managed to work with these people for over five years now, and going all crackers on them in defense of Diane wasn't going to help anyone. He still had a culvert to take care of, and he and the roads department would be getting the blame if the commissioners stalled it.

As for Diane, she probably wanted to keep this job for a while. To withstand the inevitable storms that were coming, she needed to be firm and able to stand for herself. The politicians weren't all bad, after all. But they all had their moments.

Like any other human, he decided humorously. Show him a perfect person and he'd be sure he was looking at the Blessed Mother herself. Anyway, if it became necessary, he knew a few ways to step in to make them back off her.

Inside the chamber on the second floor of the courthouse, just beneath the courtrooms and judges' chambers on the third floor, only one commissioner had arrived. Madge Corker, a graying woman of near sixty, sat in her usual chair and eyed him with a smile.

"So we have a baby with us now, Blaine?"

"If ya won't mind, I'll be letting the planner explain it herself."

"Don't go Irish on me," she said lightly. "Usually I like to listen to that accent, but when you carry it too far, I have trouble understanding. I think we need to understand today."

"No doubt," he answered, plopping himself in a seat in the front row. "I've a culvert I need to talk about. I was planning that for tonight."

A sound of amusement escaped Madge. "You were always good at diversion."

"No diversion except around that culvert. Detours."

Another sound of amusement escaped her, then two men entered, wearing pressed Western shirts and jeans. The local dress-up. If you took an iron to it, you didn't need the three-piece and tie.

Neither of them looked remotely amused. Of course not. Men had a thing about babies at work. Women in the clerk's office were still trying to get a private closet for nursing.

Jeff Holdrum, the first to enter, was a portly man, just portly enough to look well-to-do and to sport a small spot of egg yolk on the front of his shirt. Minor Allcoke was a weedy man who looked as if he'd been starving all his life. Except Blaine had more than once watched him eat as if he were a three-hundred-pound rugby player.

As the two new arrivals took their place at the council table on its dais, Blaine felt some apprehension.

"This is all looking rather official," he said. "Where are the others?"

"That's tonight. Where's Ms. Finch? She's supposed to be here."

"I gave her ten minutes." He glanced at his watch. Then, just to annoy them, he switched to an uppercrust British accent, which he seldom used. "Only seven have passed. To avoid being rude, you understand."

For a second, he enjoyed watching them look a bit embarrassed. What was it about speaking the queen's English in the queen's accent that seemed to make Americans feel a bit…scolded? He wasn't sure.

Jeff Holdrum cleared his throat. "This is just about getting to know her."

"Right-o. I thought you already interviewed her."

"Some…things have changed."

"Hell, life has a way o' doing that, don't you know." Then he folded his arms and waited. He just hoped Diane didn't begin on her back foot. Weakness didn't stand up well against these folks. Given Madge was a woman, he hoped she was here to protect Diane, but he'd also seen enough women go after other women to know better than to hope.

He felt the unmistakable change of room pressure as the door at the back opened. Three sets of eyes left him and looked to the rear. He was tempted not to look at all, but then he changed his mind.

Diane was walking up the center aisle with the baby carrier all decked out in fresh yellow in one hand, the denim diaper bag over her shoulder and a briefcase in hand. He eyed her with admiration. Not only was she lovely, she'd also been serious about putting all her cards on the table. No mistaking it. Her stride was almost defiant.

"Hello," she said. "I'm sorry if I kept you waiting." She placed the carrier on the floor and next to it the diaper bag and briefcase. Then she walked up confidently to the dais and offered her hand. "We've met before, of course," she said. "At my interview. It's nice to see you again."

She even managed to address them all by name, a feat since she had only met them once nearly two months ago.

"What can I do for you?" she asked. "I've been looking into grant resources for various projects on your list, but it would be helpful if the projects could be prioritized for me. It would also help with writing the new comprehensive plan."

Straight to business. Blaine settled back to enjoy watching Diane take charge of this entire questionable meeting.

After a moment, Madge spoke. "We'd need everyone together for that. This is a special meeting."

"I gathered." Diane smiled and took a seat close to the child and her two bags. "I'm all ears."

Madge seemed reluctant, so it was Holdrum who put his foot in the potential quicksand. "We weren't aware you had a child. I believe that was one of the questions asked on your application, about your general family situation."

"It was," Diane answered pleasantly. "But if you look at my application, you'll find I didn't answer because the question is illegal. I thought it was just a holdover that hadn't been corrected so I ignored it. Regardless, I don't see why that would be a problem. Haven't you all worked when you had children?"

Allcoke cleared his throat. "Are you just babysitting, then? For how long?"

"I'm fostering for my cousin, who is seriously ill. I will have Daphne indefinitely. Again, why would that be a problem? And why do you need to know?"

The three commissioners traded looks. "It might interfere with your work," Holdrum said, nearly swallowing his words.

"Really? I'm seeking day care for her, but even so, making an issue out of the fact that I have a child to care for strikes me as illegal. So was the question on the application which I ignored, but I wasn't inclined to make an issue at that time."

Bravo, Blaine thought. She'd just cornered them. Maybe not the best way to get off on the right foot, but no question who was holding the reins right now.

Madge at last spoke. "Apparently we're sounding like an inquisition. That isn't our intent, but tonight these questions will arise again, and we need to know if there's some way we can forestall them or at least knock them down. Trust me, I'm on your side. Fostering a child is not an easy thing to do."

No, thought Blaine. It wasn't. It was also another thing for these folks to gnash their teeth over if they chose.

Daphne chose that moment to make her presence known with a loud cry and waving arms and legs.

"Allow me," Blaine said, moving swiftly. He opened the straps holding the child safely in place and lifted her to his shoulder. "There's a good girl," he said, patting her bottom. "Feeding time?"

Diane opened the flap on the diaper bag and pulled out a bottle, removing the cover from the nipple. Blaine shifted the child to the crook of his arm and started feeding her. "Nothing like a babe to remind you of the important things," he remarked as Daphne began to suckle quietly. He gave a stern eyeball to the three people on the dais.

Just then the back door opened again, and Wyatt Carter strode in, his black judicial robe flapping around his denim-clad legs.

"Can we help you, Judge?" Allcoke asked.

"No. I'm taking a recess because I heard about this little impromptu meeting. I'm sure you don't need me to remind you that meeting without a quorum and without public notice isn't exactly… copacetic. Then I heard all this was about a baby."

He walked over to take a look at Daphne tucked so securely into Blaine's arm. "Almost as cute as my daughter, although I guess I'm prejudiced." Then he faced the commissioners again.

"You really don't want to mess with this," he said. "I can give you chapter and verse if you like, but this woman is entitled to have a child, and she's entitled since she just moved here to take a little time to find proper care for the baby. Until then, her private office will do, and I don't see how the child's presence there will disturb anyone."

Holdrum raised his hands. Allcoke looked a little red. Madge smiled almost secretly.

"We were trying to forestall any problems at the public meeting tonight," Holdrum said.

"Oh, I can make time to come tonight if you think you'll need my legal opinion. And Blaine here doesn't seem at all disturbed by holding an infant and feeding her, something I'm quite sure he volunteered to do. In fact, if I know our county engineer after these past five years, I'd place odds on him liking to have the child around."

"Amen," said Blaine. "Wasn't about to let these gob—commissioners ride roughshod over Ms. Finch, who, by the way, was doing a grand job of standing her ground."

Wyatt Carter turned to look at Diane. "I'm sorry if I got in your way, Ms. Finch. I'm quite sure you're capable of handling this matter by yourself. My wife's like that. But in my opinion, you shouldn't even have to face this." He smiled. "I guess I was premature."

Diane shook her head. "I'll stand my ground, but it's nice to have support, Judge."

"Wyatt," he corrected again. Then he turned to the commissioners. "I've held fire on this subject, but I'm aware that a number of the clerks would like to have a room set aside for nursing their children. Which just goes to show there's nothing wrong in this county with women bringing their infants to work. If you want something to argue about tonight, I suggest the nursing room would be a good topic. And remember, I hold the gavel."

Then he strode out, black robes streaming behind him.

"Wow," whispered Diane.

Blaine was pretty sure that only he heard her. He rocked the baby gently, enjoying watching her drain her bottle.

For a few minutes the commissioners remained silent. Only Madge didn't look seriously annoyed.

"Is there something else I can do for you?" Diane asked pleasantly. "It'll soon be time to change a diaper, then I'd like to get back to work on all the projects you're considering. Some will be more easily accomplished than others, but I need to be familiar with them all to write the plan and start seeking grants."

Allcoke cleared his throat. "You want a list of priorities?"

"If you can give me one. It might come down to my judgment about how quickly we can gain grant money for some of them. For example, if I can get money in six months for that scenic road, I'm sure you'd like me to do that rather than wait on a grant process that could take years."

Now heads were nodding with her.

"We'd like your assessment, Ms. Finch," Madge said. "That would be a great help to us."

"Just call me Diane, please," she said. "Very well. I'll view the proposals and ideas from the perspective of earliest funding. It might take me a few days."

Holdrum waved a hand. "Take as long as you need," he said glumly. "After all, we haven't had anyone working on this in entirely too long."

"Would you like a presentation tonight, a general outline of what I'm planning to do?"

"That would be nice," Holdrum agreed. He sighed. "I wish I'd never allowed myself to be pushed into this, Ms. Finch. I'm sorry."

"Victory," Blaine said when they returned to her office and closed the door. At once, Diane set about changing Daphne's diaper, then burping her gently with a receiving blanket thrown over her shoulder.

"The big guns certainly arrived," she said. "I never expected that."

"Well, the whole damn place has been buzzing today because everyone heard about this so-called meeting. Hardly surprising that Wyatt showed up. I'm not prepared to instruct those people on what's legal and what isn't. Not my place, and I happen to like my job. But Wyatt…well, all he did was back up what you were saying. You're allowed to have a kid. The law favors you. When *he* said so, they could hardly argue."

Diane paced the small confines of her office, loving Daphne's baby scents, loving the warmth on her shoulder. The little girl made some cooing noises, then drifted into contented sleep.

"What do you think that was all about?" she asked. "It seemed strange."

"'Twas indeed. At first I thought it was intelligence gathering, but then I had another idea when they asked the question about the application you supplied."

She stiffened a little, then forced herself to relax so as not to disturb Daphne. "As in I lied on it?"

"Perhaps. No way to be certain. But I'd sure like to know what eejit was behind it."

"Me, too."

Daphne expelled one of her adorable gas bubbles, and Diane used the edge of the receiving blanket to wipe a little milk from her mouth. "This one makes a lot of washing. I'm glad my rental has a washer and dryer. I'd go nuts trying to keep up with all this if I had to use a public laundry. Is there even one around here?"

He shook his head. "Haven't seen one. The apartment complex has laundries for its tenants, but I guess most folks around here have their own machines, however old. I hear the appliance repair guy does a booming business."

"I can easily imagine that." She continued to pace, a glance at the clock telling her it was nearly lunch hour. Well, she'd brought along a peanut butter sandwich for herself and some cucumber spears. No need to go out with the baby, something she tried to avoid because she didn't think she was ready to deal with even something as small as a cold.

Her knowledge of small children seemed ridiculously limited for a thirty-two-year-old woman. Embarrassingly paltry. For the first time in her life, she thought about getting a how-to book. *Mothering for Dummies* or something.

She glanced at Blaine and saw that he was watching her carry Daphne with a small smile on his face. "Are you missing babies or something?" she asked baldly.

He blinked, as if startled by her blunt question, then laughed. "I suppose I am. Seems like we always had one in the house needing attention."

"Most boys would have resented that." She paused. "Most girls, too, I guess."

"Me mam worked hard. Everyone pitched in what they could."

Six kids? She could well believe it. Glancing down at her shoulder, she realized Daphne had drifted off to sleep again, her little fist pressed against her mouth.

"I need to get her a playpen," she remarked. "I'm

not sure where to go, but I have no baby furniture at all." Then she switched tack abruptly. "How did the judge get involved in that meeting? And why?"

"Wyatt's a good sort," Blaine answered. "I know he's been stewing for a few months about the nursing room and trying to find a way to insert himself."

"He didn't have any trouble inserting himself a short while ago," she retorted, a tremor of amusement in her voice.

"Well, he's not the sort to be running around shoving his opinion on everyone. The commissioners gave him an excuse. I'm surprised he didn't show up with a flaming sword."

"Or gavel," she answered. She shook her head a bit. "I could have handled it."

"Sure, and weren't you doing just that? He made it clear, I thought, that you could deal with any adversaries, but he seemed to be having a problem with their little illicit meeting."

She nodded her head. "He did bring that up. Rather forcibly. But still mildly." The judge had a presence to him, she thought. As Blaine did. She doubted very many messed with either of them.

"Well, I need to be getting out there to meet with a man who wants to do some work on his storefront. I don't know if you've gotten around to reading all that stuff yet, but we *do* have historical preservation ordinances. Gotta make sure he doesn't get too carried away."

"Thanks for everything, Blaine."

"No thanks needed. I had a culvert to talk about, and somehow we never got around to it. Not that it matters, since the meeting never happened."

She wondered if he were giving her some advice in that last statement. It wouldn't surprise her. Getting those commissioners into trouble wouldn't be a very good way to start out, and even the judge had merely warned them.

The door closed behind Blaine, and she decided that she might as well get some work done before Daphne woke up again. She seemed more active during the day now that the confusion level had died down a bit. Diane could only suppose that was good. A baby couldn't possibly sleep all the time, but it would be awfully nice if she weren't awake a lot at night.

After she'd settled Daphne into the carrier, she sat at her desk again and studied the heap of folders. She needed to get that mess—it was a mess, looking like a long-accreting wish list that might be only marginally useful—onto a computer, where she could organize everything by likelihood of a grant and likelihood of ever completing it, then nail down the folks involved about what they really wanted.

Because somehow at least some of this had to be incorporated into the plan when she was getting that straight with all the newer state and federal environmental regulations.

Blaine was going to talk to a guy about his historical facade? The county engineer? Didn't they have someone to handle that?

Remembering the list she'd seen in one of her drawers, she pulled it out and began to scan names. The date at the top said it was recent, but nowhere did she see anyone in charge of following the historic district rules. Or many rules, come to that. She wondered if that would now fall to her, as it apparently had to Blaine.

One of the downsides to a small rural area, she supposed. Well, she'd wanted more authority and responsibility. It appeared she was about to get it.

Then she looked at the stack of papers again. Damn, she needed an assistant to help get all this stuff into some kind of order. To get it on a computer where she could edit and rearrange easily.

Because she wasn't just taking over for someone who'd kept everything up-to-date. Nope, she was on an archaeological expedition.

Chapter Four

The meeting with the full city council and commission went off without a hitch, and Diane even got permission to hire an assistant and was offered an adjoining office. She suspected that Judge Wyatt Carter's appearance earlier had put them all on their best behavior. Not a peep about Daphne, either.

By Friday evening, she'd finished unpacking as much as she could, and took inventory of what she still needed. A chest of drawers would be very useful. A changing table. A playpen that could double as a crib unless she found one she really liked. Some more baby clothes, because at the rate she was going, she'd wear out the washer and dryer on small loads.

Daphne hadn't come to her with very much, and she hadn't had a whole lot of time to take care of shopping for her. The social worker had helped her over the first few steps—the car seat, the diaper bag, the set of bottles and formula—but then she'd been on her own, and there hadn't been much she could do until now.

Nor did she have any idea where to shop or even if she could find what was needed in this town. At that moment, Daphne was wiggling and proving that a receiving blanket wasn't big enough to create boundaries for her.

At least the floor was wood. That could be lightly mopped and kept clean. If this place had been carpeted, she wouldn't have dared put the baby down on it, at least not until after one heck of a steam cleaning.

Leaning back in her recliner without lifting the footrest, she watched Daphne with fascination. This little life was absorbing more and more of her attention, something she hadn't expected. All day long, even while she was working and Daphne was sleeping, thoughts of the baby danced around in the back of her mind. It was, she thought with amusement, exactly like the early days of a love affair.

Daphne was creeping—at least Diane thought that's what it was. She'd wiggled from side to side, pushing with her legs. The blanket wasn't exactly helping her, but it wasn't hindering her much, either. So much effort to move a few inches.

Then Daphne reared up, pushing downward with her arms, and startled herself by rolling over. She'd been doing that all along, at least since Diane had received her, but this time she proved not to be at all pleased by the change of view.

She let out a loud cry and her face turned red as she waved her arms.

"I guess you need to learn to turn over again when you want to," Diane said with a laugh. Rising, she gently rolled Daphne. At once the incipient temper tantrum calmed. The girl evidently had places she wanted to go. She resumed creeping, only to stop a minute later, close her eyes and fall asleep.

Such a peaceful scene. Amazing how beautiful a sleeping child could be.

The buzz of her cell phone, resting on the box she was using as an end table, surprised her. She reached for it mostly out of habit. She hadn't been here long enough to create friendships, and her friends from the past usually called on Sunday afternoon when no one was too busy to talk.

She answered, expecting a sales call of some kind.

"Hi," said Blaine Harrigan. "You were speaking of baby furniture. Freitag's is open late tonight, it being Friday and all. Would you and the tot like to look around? Plus," he added, a hint of amusement in his tone, "I'm blessed with a chariot big enough to transport any items you might decide to bring home."

Diane, who'd just been settling in for a relaxing evening with Daphne and a book, felt a leap of pleasure. An evening with Blaine was bound to be better than a book, and Daphne might actually enjoy the stimulation. For all she didn't want to expose the baby to some illness, the child *did* need to see and experience something besides an office and a living room.

And lately all kinds of things had been dancing through her mind, things like a mobile for the baby to watch, little toys she could grab and gnaw on...

"Oh, yes, I'd love that!" Her answer was enthusiastic, but she honestly didn't know whether her enthusiasm was more for shopping or for being out with Blaine.

She guessed it didn't matter, though. She not only had a new job and a new baby, but she also had a new life to build. Friends made any locale a far more enjoyable place to live.

Although, she thought as she picked Daphne up in order to change her and dress her more warmly for the outing, the baby would probably limit her social life for a while.

That was okay, she thought as she snuggled the warm little body close. This mother thing was okay, more okay than she'd expected.

Blaine had been so busy with the culvert and a number of other issues that seemed to spring up like weeds that he'd hardly seen Diane since the day of the meeting.

But that didn't mean she'd been out of mind while she was out of sight. No, she rather haunted him like a wraith at the edge of his mind.

No, not a wraith, he corrected himself. Damn, the Irish in him was getting the better of his thoughts. A wraith wasn't a good thing. In fact, the idea of a wraith could make a chill run down his spine, and he didn't hold himself to be especially superstitious.

But Diane had been haunting his thoughts, popping up unexpectedly at odd moments, accompanied by an impulse to go see her. It had been years since a woman had reached him that way, an occasion he didn't like to remember because he'd been young and callow and had made an utter arse of himself. Anyone with a hair of sense would have realized she wasn't interested, that she was merely patting him on the head like a puppy.

He'd survived that and put it in the past, but he hoped he was wiser now. He was certainly older. But there was no escaping the way Diane appealed to him. Easy enough to handle, he assured himself. And right now all he was doing was helping a new coworker settle in.

He dumped all the maps from the back seat of his SUV into the cargo area to make it ready for Daphne's car seat. It was going to be just like old times, putting a car seat in a car.

The coming autumn was putting a bit of nip in the evening air, so he closed the car door before going to get Diane.

She opened the door immediately, and the smile she gave him suggested that she might have been dealing with a bit of cabin fever. Well, she'd hardly had a chance to do anything except work and care for the babe. She was hunting for an assistant, but every time he popped his head into her office, she'd been buried in files, tapping at her computer or changing a diaper. Not much of a life for such a fine young woman who didn't have any help at home.

The baby was already in her car seat and covered by a light receiving blanket. Blaine took her and peeked under the blanket. "Sure and she's growing."

Diane laughed. "Her clothes certainly say so."

The drive to Freitag's Mercantile wasn't a long one. "Well, nothing in this town is much of a drive from anywhere else," Blaine said. "Freitag's goes back to the earliest days of this town. I hope you're liking creaky wood floors and crammed space. I'm thinking we should carry Daphne in without the seat."

"That crowded, huh?"

"Loaded with all sorts of good stuff. I think the owner's trying to prevent people from driving to bigger cities."

Diane laughed. "A noble goal. Business stays at home, then jobs stay at home."

"I'm in the way of thinking some of the salespeople in there have had those jobs since Freitag's opened."

A laugh spilled from Diane again, this time freer and more comfortable than the first.

She climbed out without his assistance and opened the rear door, disturbing Daphne as she removed her from her seat. "Come on, sweetheart, we've got all kinds of new things to look at."

Indeed, thought Blaine as he took charge of the diaper bag.

Woman and child walking into the store. An iconic image, he thought, despite the modern clothes. Damn, he was turning sappy, a questionable thing for an engineer. Logic. Science.

And a woman and a baby.

Laughing at himself, he walked into Freitag's behind her. Daphne was awake, bright little eyes hopping around, one fist against her mouth. He wondered how long it would be before all the unaccustomed stimulus overwhelmed her.

The baby merchandise was all stashed in a large alcove at the rear of the store. It wasn't the biggest selection, but it was adequate for whatever Diane might consider to be her immediate needs.

Rubbing Daphne's back, Diane began to wander around looking at everything. "Changing table," she remarked.

"Useful," he agreed. "Mam used an old chest of drawers. After six babies it didn't look very grand."

Diane laughed again, quietly. Daphne apparently liked the sound, because she began to coo. Diane shifted the girl into the cradle of her left arm.

"Here, let me hold her," Blaine said. "It'll be easier for you to look around."

Diane turned to him without reluctance and passed Daphne to him. He understood what a compliment that was. He had already noted how closely attached she was becoming to the child, and many mothers were reluctant to put a child so young in a virtual stranger's arms.

Once Diane made up her mind what she was going to do, Blaine went to find a clerk to help organize it all. Soon the back of his SUV was loaded with boxes containing a crib, a changing table and a playpen. Diane hesitated over the high chair, then decided it could wait a bit.

After that it was several bags of infant clothes, some washcloths and other necessities. A whole layette, basically, something Daphne hadn't come with.

Watching Diane give herself over wholeheartedly to providing her small cousin's needs, he smiled. The little one had no idea how fortunate she was. Diane was throwing her heart and soul into this.

The last purchase was a musical mobile, with colorful soft shapes hanging from it. Then Diane passed over her credit card and didn't even wince when she saw the total.

"Let me move all the boxes inside," Blaine suggested as they reached her house once again. "I can come over tomorrow and help with the assembly. You'll be happier once things are set up to your liking."

Diane made an amused sound. "Next I guess I'll need to shop for my own furniture. Not much came with the place. Anyway, with Daphne creeping now,

I need ways to keep her confined so I can go cook a dinner or something. I can't watch her every minute."

"That's what we have ears for."

He felt her look at him as he pulled up in front of the house. "Meaning?"

"You'll discover as she gets older especially that your ears are better nannies than your eyes."

"Right now," Diane answered, "my ears are telling me that she's getting cranky and hungry and probably needs a diaper change."

For certain, the noises from the back were sounding less like the coos she'd been making at the store and more like *Will someone please pay attention?*

"You take charge of the baby," Blaine said as he switched off the ignition. "I'll bring in the purchases. Just wave me through to where you want them."

"That's an awful lot to carry," she said as she opened her door and put one foot to the ground. "I'll help as soon as I settle Daphne."

"Not to worry. I've a strong back and I've carried more than that in my life. Loads of brick, in fact, when I was studying engineering."

"That's a story I want to hear," she said.

"And leave the car seat. I'll get that, too."

For the first time he passed the nearly vacant front room and kitchen. There were two small bedrooms in the back, and Diane told him to take everything to the one on the right. As he carried in the boxes and bags, it seemed to him that this small bedroom was about to become very crowded. Well, he supposed she'd want the playpen up front, but still, it would be a squeeze to fit the crib, the changing table and the small chest she'd bought. And the room didn't have a closet!

He was used to that at home. That was why armoires had been created, but even if he'd had one, it wouldn't fit here. He paused, using his skills to envision the best layout so Diane wouldn't be tripping over herself trying to move in here.

A glance in the other bedroom, the one she occupied, suggested it wasn't much bigger.

Well, space wasn't a problem he could solve in this rental house.

Diane had changed Daphne's nappy on the living room floor atop a blanket, and now she was feeding the babe, who at last appeared content. And alert. That girl seemed like she didn't want to miss a thing. From time to time, she released the nipple and made little vocalizations that almost sounded as if she were talking. Then she'd go back to her bottle, her eyes fixed on Diane.

"So," he said as he looked around, "how long are you planning to live as a minimalist?"

Diane shook her head a little, but she wasn't frowning. "Most of what I had before came from a secondhand shop, and I don't mean an upscale one. I also relied on boxes to be tables. I never intended to stay forever in Des Moines, so I furnished as little as possible, and hardly any of it was worth bringing with me. Saves a lot on moving costs. This chair is the only piece of furniture I actually brought with me."

He dropped onto the floor and sat cross-legged, elbows on his knees. "Might make entertaining a few friends difficult." He was glad that she chuckled quietly.

"It might," she admitted. "I realize I have to get at least a few things." She paused. "I can't stop thinking about how the judge charged into that meeting the other morning."

Blaine tilted his head. "I can't say I expected it. However, Wyatt Carter is a straight arrow, and it probably chapped him a bit to hear about some of the commissioners meeting without public notice. I think I mentioned that to you. And then there's the whole thing about a nursing room for the mothers who work in the courthouse. That's been hemmed and hawed about for a year. Maybe more," he said after a moment. "Be that as it may, you wouldn't think the politicians would find it all that difficult. A small room, a chair or two. Oh, and a lightbulb."

She giggled softly. "You make it sound so easy, but it turns the patriarchy upside down."

"Now how could that be?" he said. "None of the patriarchy would exist without a mother who nursed them."

"Maybe that's what gets to them."

"Hmm." He rubbed his chin. "Well, whatever made them stubborn, I know it was irritating more than the clerks. Wyatt was getting irritated by the way it was dragging on, but it was wholly under the purview of the powers that be. Namely commissioners and councilmen who sometimes can be too stubborn for no discernible reason. And why it should all fall to them anyway, beats me. Seriously? The janitor could have just made them the room, and who would have argued about it then?"

Diane was now grinning. Daphne appeared to be done with her bottle, so Diane laid her tummy down across her knees and rubbed gently while the child reached for invisible objects, stretching her arms and opening and closing her tiny hands. The soft coos and trills had returned. Soon they'd be followed by sleepiness.

"You want me to put that playpen together for you tonight?" Blaine asked.

"I don't think there's a rush. But thank you. In fact, thank you for everything you've done tonight."

He waved his hand, indicating it was of no importance.

"How is the culvert going?" she asked as she placed Daphne on her receiving blanket to inch her way around until sleep found her. A small soft toy was there for her to grab, but Blaine, without answering her question, stretched out near the blanket's edge and dangled a key ring, causing it to make a quiet ringing sound.

At once Daphne arched her back to look.

"I won't let her grab them," Blaine said. "I hate to think of how much grime they have on them."

"I'm not worried," Diane answered. She'd had Daphne long enough now to realize that sterility was an impossible ideal. The girl would put anything in her mouth, including a dead fly a few days ago. She was still healthy.

And she was fascinated by the keys. With great effort and focus, she pushed herself toward them.

All of a sudden Blaine stood up. "I have a better idea."

Diane watched him stride toward the back of the house and returned her attention to Daphne. A better idea?

A few minutes later, she had her answer as Blaine set up the playpen, an easy task since basically it just needed to be folded open and locked. Then he clamped the mobile on and started it playing.

Daphne was scooped up with her blanket and settled in the playpen on her back, where she became instantly fascinated by the mobile and its slowly turning brightly colored shapes of stars, fishes and cats. An eclectic assortment, Diane thought with amusement.

Then Blaine disappeared again and returned with one of the paper bags she'd brought home. This one contained not clothing but toys. Cute little toys she hadn't been able to resist, items for Daphne to gnaw on, grasp and eventually throw, she guessed.

Satisfied at last, Blaine returned to his cross-legged position on the floor. "Now," he said, "you can run to the loo or take a shower without having to straitjacket her in her car seat."

Diane laughed. "How did you know what I was doing?"

"I told you, I was the eldest of six. I had to practice all kinds of devious methods to get a moment or two to myself."

She looked at him there, sitting on her floor with his arm draped over one upraised knee, and began to feel like a very bad hostess. "You've helped me so much and I haven't even offered you coffee or tea."

He shook his head, one corner of his mouth lifting. "I don't recall asking for anything. Besides, I'm enjoying myself. I miss my family. This is kind of making up for it."

A tingle of unease settled in her stomach, but she couldn't have said why. "Are you thinking about moving back home?"

"In the foreseeable future? Nah. The youngest is grown-up, me mam has found a new man and there's not much need for me at home. My visiting is enough. Besides, I believe I told you I like it here."

So he wasn't leaving. Why that should matter to her…well, she didn't want to think about that. She'd known the man less than a week. Bad enough that she thought about him at odd moments and felt her feminine side weakening with desire. Nothing worse, she reminded herself, than getting involved with a coworker.

"What about you?" he asked. "You told me your cousin is sick, but is there no one else?"

Diane focused her gaze on Daphne, who seemed to have fallen asleep despite all the new distractions. Or maybe because of them. A trip to the store that had kept her wide-awake with fascination, and now the new toys and mobile. She reminded herself that she needed to keep the girl stimulated. Dang, she had missed the mother genes, evidently. Come to the game unprepared. Daphne wasn't a doll who could be tucked into a corner. She needed a whole lot to keep her thriving.

"Diane? Bad question?"

She sighed. "I don't want to advertise this."

"I'm not given to gossip, if that's what you're meaning. I may listen, but I seldom repeat unless it's something casual and harmless."

She hesitated a little longer, then decided life would probably be easier if she had a confidant. Lately life had been overwhelming her, and even with her old girlfriends she'd felt it wisest to just put a bright face on everything. She hadn't even told them what was wrong with MaryJo.

"I'll be honest, Blaine. There are some things in society that are considered…" How could she even explain it? "Shameful?" She tried that on, then left it. "It's unfair, but that's the way people react."

He nodded slowly. "And that would be?"

"My cousin is a paranoid schizophrenic, and she

was hospitalized because she doesn't respond to drug therapy."

"She's out of her blazing mind, then."

Diane compressed her lips, feeling a spark of anger but unable to deny what he said. "You could put it that way."

He shook his head and stood up. "I don't mean that in a bad sense. Sometimes I'm too blunt for my own good." He paced a couple of steps then came back. "You have a teapot? And a box of loose tea?"

"Teapot yes, loose tea, no."

"Then I suggest we repair to the kitchen where there are two chairs and have a bit of tea, the inevitable cure for everything in my homeland."

"Britain, too, I guess," she said, smiling wanly.

"We don't mention them. Too many bad memories still in the air." But he spoke pleasantly, not at all critically.

She checked Daphne again, but the child was happily sleeping, so she followed Blaine into the kitchen.

"Tell me where to find everything?" he asked.

So she pointed out what little she had, then settled down to let him make the tea as he chose.

"Your cousin is that ill, then. Not much hope, I expect?"

"They weren't offering any."

"No other family?"

Another question she hated to answer. "Her father disappeared before she was born, and her mother was an alcoholic."

"Was?" He set the kettle on to boil and opened the box of tea bags. From the overhead cupboard, he pulled down her Japanese teapot with the wicker handle. "I like these," he said, indicating the pot. "Was?" he repeated.

"MaryJo's parents—well, that's a strange story. They split when MaryJo was little. She never saw her father again. Her mother became an alcoholic, which didn't help anything. Anyway, a couple of years ago, the two of them got together briefly in Texas. No one knows why they met up and probably never will, but while they were there, the two of them drowned in a flash flood."

"Good God," he said. "That must have been devastating for your cousin. And how strange they got together!" He shook his head a bit as he moved around the kitchen. "Will I ever understand people?"

"I don't know. It's sad, but my family had little contact with hers. I'm not sure why. I guess the situation turned them off. Anyway, my parents moved a lot and seldom went back to Gillette—my dad was in the oil business and…any ties just evaporated. I sent MaryJo Christmas cards. Does that make me awful?"

He leaned back against the counter, waiting for the kettle to boil. "No. Families are created by blood. Not by choice. Sometimes they don't work out. With as little contact as you had with your cousin, she's a stranger, isn't she?"

"Unfortunately. Or maybe fortunately. I don't know." Diane looked down, feeling a wave of guilt accompanied by some grief. The fact that she didn't know MaryJo didn't make her feel a whole lot better.

"So that left you to take care of the daffodil," he said. He arranged tea bags in the pot, the tags hanging out, and poured boiling water into it. Along with a couple of cups, he set it on the table then sat across from her.

"You're awfully alone," he remarked. "At least in terms of people who might help you with the babe."

"I knew that would be the case when I took this on." She put her chin in her hand, just looking at him because he was so easy on the eyes, and realized that her ears were tuned toward the living room, listening for Daphne sounds. "You called her daffodil?"

"Better than Daffy."

That drew a tired laugh from her. "True that."

"But back to you," he said. "Taking on a baby is huge. It's not like you were eagerly awaiting a bundle of joy and taking parenting classes or whatever. It must have been sudden."

"It was. But I couldn't do anything else, Blaine. When that social worker started talking about putting Daphne in foster care, it was like everything inside me shriveled. And there wasn't even a chance she could be adopted into a good home, because my cousin isn't well enough to give her up, so that would involve all kinds of court hearings that might drag on for years. The only thing I was sure of was that I couldn't let Daphne be handed over to strangers.

They might have been nice strangers, but…at least I know the kind of person I am."

"A kindhearted one," he said decisively. He poured tea into their cups then lifted his for a sip. "Ah," he said.

"The tea bags worked?"

"They did. Like I said, I'm not some kind of connoisseur. I'm a man on my own, and when I'm in a hurry, I'm not picky."

She watched him. He closed his eyes, savoring the tea, the lines of his face relaxing somewhat. All the while she watched, she felt as if her entire being were being pulled toward him.

Gah! she thought and tore her gaze away. A handsome Irishman was *not* going to turn her into a puddle. She couldn't allow it. Too much settling in to do on the job. Too much she needed to learn about being a good mother for Daphne.

"How's the culvert project?" she asked for the second time, seeking safe ground.

"Ah, well." He set his cup down and refilled it from the pot. "The plans are being drawn up. I'm working with the roads department to see if we can come up with something more durable, but given the climate hereabouts, I doubt it. We'll try anyway, because the detour already has a half dozen ranchers climbing our backs. It adds quite a few miles for them to get to town. Be that as it may, chances are we'll use the concrete culverts we already have at the lot, sink another galvanized steel pipe in for extra reinforcement and once again wait for nature to do its work."

Diane felt a bubble of amusement. "Isn't that always the way with roads?"

"Aye, but I can hope. I mean, I keep thinking of the Appian Way, two thousand years of foot and cart traffic. And there are roads in Mexico and Peru that are centuries old."

"Dream big, do you?"

He unleashed a laugh that seem to rise from the depths of his being. "Guilty."

He'd been likable from the start, but in that instant she knew she liked him above average. A glance at the clock told her Daphne would probably give her an hour before waking again, and Blaine seemed in no hurry to leave.

Not that she wanted him to. His company was pleasant, calming in a way. But exciting, too. It was that exciting part that worried her.

"I told you my mother, otherwise known as Mam, got herself a new man."

Diane's interest pricked immediately. "I don't remember. Is that a problem?"

"Not for her, I gather. I only go home once a year." He leaned forward, resting his elbows on the table. "What concerns me is the very strong feeling I get that he'd rather I not show up at all. Now, there's no reason for him to be jealous of me. I'm hardly there. But I find myself wondering what is it he doesn't want me to know or find out."

Diane drew a sharp breath. "Oh, Blaine, really? But what about your other brothers and sisters? Surely they'd have noticed if something was wrong?"

He shook his head. "They're scattered all over the EU now. You go where the jobs are. So Mam is essentially on her own in Galway."

Diane resisted an urge to reach out for his hand. "Friends? She must have friends."

"She certainly used to. Neighbors have moved away over the years, but there was always church. My mother was one of those who had a string of rosary beads in her hand most of the time, went to Mass every single morning, did a lot with parish events."

Diane nodded slowly. "And now?"

"Not so much. I asked her last time I was there, what about church? Daily Mass? She said she went when she felt like it. That doesn't sound like her. I asked the others to check it out, but they're not seeing any more than I am. Mam's lost interest in the church. She wouldn't be the only Irish person to do that since the scandals, but her faith was something different. At least I thought it was."

Diane bit her lip. "Could she be ill?"

"She doesn't appear to be. And I might be over-reacting since I'm so far away. Natural, maybe, that when a new man appears in your mother's life you get a little uneasy."

Diane could understand his worry. The situation

would generate concern. "Have you tried talking to her about it?"

He tilted his head. "I believe we all have. She insists she's quite happy. I'm probably worrying entirely too much. She hasn't married the bloke, and the family silver is still in the drawer where she's always kept it. It's likely everything is fine and there's no reason for any of us to wonder about it. Perhaps we're all just having trouble seeing a stranger where Da used to be."

She nodded, thinking it over. Of course, she knew nothing at all about the real situation, so what did she have to offer? A word of sympathy? Then something he had said struck her. "You have family silver?"

A grin slashed across his face. "Sounds all important like, doesn't it? Like we must be descended from landed gents or something. But it's just a few small tarnished pieces, come down through generations and no one knows from where. Maybe an ancestor who worked in one of the grand English houses as a maid and lifted a piece from time to time."

"Oh, I like that story."

He laughed. "Believe me, it's the likeliest way a Harrigan could have come by some silver." He rose. "I've got to be on my way, Ms. Finch. There's a darts game waiting for me at the pub...er, bar, and I mustn't be late. Shall I come by in the morning to help with the rest of the furniture?"

It had taken Blaine a while to settle into Conard County. As friendly as the place was, like in many small communities, you needed to be around for a while to be accepted as a local—or rather, *almost* a local. He fancied he might just be arriving at that exalted place.

He hoped he was helping ease Diane's way into all this. Remarkable woman, he thought, not for the first time. Not so much for deciding to take on this position and moving here to the middle of everything— or the middle of nowhere, depending on your measure. No, what impressed him was that she'd so readily taken on her cousin's child, and at the most inconvenient time imaginable, just as she was starting a new job and having to move away from everyone she knew.

Of course, it probably helped her admirability factor that she displayed such an attractive bundle of curves.

That was a thought he quashed quickly, steering away from it with long practice. If he wanted a woman, it would be best to look far enough away that no one here would know about it, unless he was prepared to ignore the constant interest from the local denizens.

He'd experienced his share of that in Galway. 'twas a big enough city, but within it were smaller communities who'd lived together for generations. Hard to keep any secret there, and hard to ignore all the unwanted advice.

There was still some feuding left over from the days when the place had been ruled by the tribes.

Wealthy, powerful and…aw, to hell with it. To this day people traded on their relationship with one tribe or another.

A certain drawer with silver in it might even go back to all that.

But as he climbed out of his vehicle and strode toward Mahoney's, he pushed away thoughts of home. Darts tonight, after a pleasant evening spent with a pleasant young woman and her darling babe… Could a man ask for much more?

Oh, yeah, he thought as he pulled the door open and the sound of voices and music poured out along with the familiar scent of stale beer and even some smoke. A man could ask for a whole lot more.

He just hadn't been in the asking mood for a very long time.

Not since Ailis. Nor did he want to be thinking of that woman right now.

He'd barely crossed the threshold before a green bottle of chilled ale was thrust into his hand, and Dan Casey, a local deputy, was urging him toward the group gathered at tables around the dartboard. He was greeted with waves of the hand and voices asking where the hell he'd been. Most of the men he played darts with were county employees, whether sheriff's deputies or road workers or firemen. It made for some interesting conversation to go with a couple of late-night beers. They usually shut the place down around one in the morning.

Like back at home. Here he truly felt the comfort

of long familiarity, as if he were at his local pub in Galway.

With one difference. He had his own very expensive set of tungsten-tipped darts. He'd never been able to afford them before, but now he could. When he pulled the black leather case out of his hip pocket, he heard Jake Madison say, "Ooh, look out now. The man's come fully armed."

Loud laughter ran around the room, and Blaine returned it with a grin. "Been sharpening my points, you gobboxes. We're ready to go."

Except that Diane kept drifting through his thoughts, her and the baby, and his concentration failed him from time to time.

He wasn't going home the winner tonight. Nor did he care.

Chapter Five

Saturday morning.

Rising early because he'd promised to put together some baby furniture today, Blaine stopped by the diner to rustle up a couple of breakfasts that included cinnamon rolls, a box of buttered toast just in case and a couple of tall lattes. He liked a coffee from time to time himself, and he suspected Diane did, as well. Something about the way she made tea persuaded him that the drip coffeemaker on her counter probably wasn't there for show.

Maude's daughter Mavis, a clone of her mother, put the takeout in a bag for him and sent him on his way.

This morning, the nip of early autumn had at last

arrived. He enjoyed the crisp air and freely admitted he didn't always miss the grayer, wetter and cooler climate in which he'd grown up. Oh, he missed going on out the fishing boat sometimes, and spending a hard day bringing in a catch they could sell. His two brothers had leased out their da's boat to a family they'd grown up with. The Quinns. Hard, dangerous work was fishing, and the seas the more dangerous for being so far north in strong currents. The Quinn boys were working their butts off, but according to his brother Liam, they were only a couple of years from paying the boat off. Good on 'em.

In some ways life had been harder back when his family depended on fishing, but better, too. There'd even occasionally been enough extra money for all the kids to go to the flicks. What grand times those had been.

He was halfway to Diane's little house when his cell rang. Dang, he hoped it wasn't something urgent, but a quick glance told him it was Diane. All right, then. He'd be there in three minutes, so no point pulling over to answer. He wondered if she wanted to postpone for some reason.

He was smiling as he knocked on Diane's door. When it opened his jaw dropped a bit. Her hair was going every which way, her robe was belted crookedly and in the crook of her arm was a rigid, screaming, red-faced Daphne.

"What happened?" he asked.

"I don't know."

Forget an invitation. He moved inside, causing her to step back. "I'll just put the breakfast and coffee on the table, shall I? Then you tell me what that child is doing."

"Screaming," she said as she followed him into the kitchen. "I don't know, Blaine. She woke me up shortly after six, and I haven't been able to figure out anything to calm her. Diaper change didn't help, she didn't want to eat when I offered the bottle, I'm not sure if she feels warm or if that's just the screaming. I'm worried."

He turned. "I gather." If he hadn't seen it in her face, he'd have recognized it in her voice. Tight with apprehension. Edged with exhaustion. Then he reached out and took Daphne from her. The girl's stiffness shook him a bit, too, but it wasn't the first time he'd seen an infant resemble a post. Any serious discomfort could do that, but it didn't always mean anything bad.

A series of questions needed answering. "How was her stool? Unusual in any way?"

Apparently such discussions were new to her, because her eyes widened and her jaw dropped a shade. If Daphne hadn't been so distressed, he might have laughed. "You've got three forms of communication with an infant, Diane—what exactly is coming out of either end and are they screaming like bloody hell. Let's start with the bottom. We already know about the screaming."

"Her diaper seemed normal. But this morning it's

like she's been constipated, maybe? Straining? But I can't be sure, Blaine! I've only had her for a little more than a week. Maybe she has screaming spells periodically."

He nodded, shifting Daphne from the crook of his arm to his shoulder, where he patted her. Her screaming was loud enough to make him wonder how much hearing he'd lose. Of course, he'd been screamed at like this before. "No vomit?"

"Nothing."

He held Daphne away from him for a few seconds, studying her. Her little feet sawed the air, and her fists waved. "She sure does look angry. Mostly miserable."

He hesitated as he pulled the baby close to his shoulder again. He was about to scare Diane to death, he supposed, but no way around it. "Get dressed and put something warm on her. We'll go to the emergency room." He braced, half expecting an explosion of anguish. Of course, his mam had always been good at going over the top. Diane surprised him.

"You think it's that bad?" Diane asked, her voice cracking.

Using his free arm, he pulled her close to his side and kept his voice as soothing as he could make it. "I don't know what's going on, so we'd be best to check it out. You said she's been crying for hours. That's not usual unless she's been colicky, and in the space of a week, I'd think you would have seen that at least once before. But I'm not a doctor, and I believe that visiting one might make all three of us feel better." At least that was his hope. But this sure didn't sound like colicky crying to him. He'd had two brothers with it.

Diane nodded, fright giving way to the need for action. "Yes, of course. God, I've never felt so helpless in my life!"

Blaine watched her turn to go get swaddling for the baby and asked, "After you dress, would you mind grabbing the two coffees I brought? I don't have any idea how long this will take."

And a coffee might be just the thing for both of them. He rocked Daphne, trying to ease her misery and completely failing. This must be why Diane had called him a little while ago. Inexperienced with a baby crying like this? She must indeed have felt helpless.

'Twas a fact—little could make a human feel as helpless as a crying babe that couldn't be soothed. Or wear one out as fast.

Strapping Daphne into her car seat was a battle. The girl was rigid as a board and fought every attempt to bend her even a little.

"The hospital is close?" Diane asked, a tremor in her voice.

"A few minutes by car. The babe won't have to endure the seat for long."

At last they got her secured, then Diane slid into the front seat beside Blaine and they took off through the quiet Saturday morning at speeds that should have gotten them a ticket. Although, thought Blaine, if any cop stopped them, one listen to Daphne's distressed crying would probably get them an escort to the hospital.

He didn't want to let Diane know, but he was worried, too. He'd helped his mam raise two colicky babies, and that uproar had a way of beginning in the evening, not in the wee hours, although he supposed it was possible. But to go this long without having seen it once? Not likely. His experience with colic had taught him it usually occurred several times a week. Could a child develop colic at three months? For that he had no idea.

Anything was possible, he supposed, but he had just run smack into the limits of his knowledge of babies. Plus, Daphne's crying didn't hold the fussy sounds of a colicky kid. It sounded pained, and that was sufficient cause for worry on a Saturday morning when the only place to go was the emergency room.

Sufficient cause to feel huge relief when he at last pulled up beside the emergency room entrance at Memorial Hospital.

"You just go ahead and take her in," he told Diane. "I'll park and come find you."

Diane lifted the shrieking Daphne out of her car seat and held her close as she hurried through the emergency room doors. Unprepared. Inexperienced. *What that hell am I doing being someone's mother?*

The mental self-kicking at least eased the fear

that lurked in every corner of her mind. This baby depended on her, and she was helpless. *Helpless.* Oh, God, she should never have taken this on. An experienced foster mother would know what to do.

But she didn't regret accepting Daphne. She looked down into that scrunched-up, reddened face and all she could feel was love and a need to get her help. Stiff as a board. Oh, God, the child was stiff as a board. That had to mean awful pain, right?

All of a sudden, she was in the middle of a swirl of people in blue scrubs. Apparently Daphne's screaming sounded like a problem to them, as well.

"How long as this been going on?" a woman asked.

"Since shortly after six. She won't eat."

"No vomiting?"

"No."

At the center of the whirlwind, she was ushered into a cubicle.

"The doctor will be here shortly," said the pleasant woman. "In the meantime I'm going to have someone come in to take your information." Then she paused and laid her hand on Diane's shoulder. "Relax. She sounds far too strong to be in imminent danger, okay? Dr. Dave will get her feeling better just as soon as he can. And if you need me, my name is Mary."

Mary was quickly replaced by a young woman pushing a cart with a computer on it. The questions began to come, but before the admission was complete, Mary returned and took Daphne from her arms.

Diane had the worst urge to cry out, *Don't take her from me.*

But that would help nothing. Steeling herself, she let go of the baby, feeling as if her skin had been ripped away.

Mary placed her on the bed with the sides up and began to unwrap her. "Screaming like this will drive you nuts," she said cheerfully. "I know, I have a couple of my own. I wasn't sure if both of us would survive the colic." She flashed a smile at Diane.

"You think it's colic?"

"First off, I'm not the doctor, so I can't say anything. But the baby..." She looked at Diane again.

"Daphne."

"Daphne's going to get the best care. I'm just going to take her temperature."

Then came the rest of the questions from the woman with the cart. The insurance part shut down the instant Diane said she was working for the county government. No ID required. They didn't even ask if Daphne was her legal daughter. She'd deal with that later. Right now, helping the baby was all that mattered.

With Daphne stripped down to her tiny undershirt, her diaper gone, Mary used the thermometer with practiced ease.

"No fever," she announced. "That's good." She wrapped the babe tightly in a blanket. "It makes infants feel more secure to be tightly wrapped. It's not going to help much right now, obviously, but a tip for another time."

"Thank you." Diane leaned back in the uncomfortable plastic chair, fatigue trying to overwhelm her even as she felt as if she were dangling over a cliff edge in fear. Daphne was still screaming and stiffening as if trying to push something away.

No, that wasn't normal, she thought. It couldn't be. She should have come here a couple of hours ago when she had begun to realize she couldn't make the baby feel any better.

Failure. The word popped up in her head. It wasn't exactly unfamiliar. She'd grown up with it. Then there had been Max. He'd been quick to fling that word around, too. She failed at everything, from cooking to cleaning.

And now she was failing Daphne. A shudder ran through her, and her eyes felt as if they were burning holes in her head.

Minutes dragged. Blaine arrived, standing to one side behind her, his hand welcome on her shoulder.

Then a man swept into the room, stethoscope hanging around his neck. "Hey, Mary, what are we looking at?"

"Screaming for about four hours, stiffening and pushing, no vomiting, no fever, and despite all that pushing, she hasn't moved any stool."

"All right."

Diane watched anxiously as the doctor pulled the

blanket away and began to press gently on Daphne's tummy. "Some rigidity," he remarked. Mary typed it in on the computer near the head of the bed.

Then he pulled his stethoscope off his shoulder and put the earpieces in his ears. He clasped the diaphragm between his gloved hands for a minute, probably warming it up, then pressed it to Daphne's tummy, listening. He moved the diaphragm around, pausing to listen again and again.

"Bowel sounds are sluggish. Something's slowing up the works."

Diane bit her lip, trying to imagine what that might mean. The exam continued, occasional words being passed to Mary for the chart. At no point did Daphne's crying ease. It was a wonder she didn't become silent out of sheer exhaustion.

Then the doctor pulled the ear stems free and leaned over Daphne, running his hands gently over her, from the top of her tummy down to her groin.

"Ah," he said, straightening. "Mom, you want to come see this?"

Diane leaped to her feet. What had he seen? She hadn't noticed anything in all these hours, and she'd changed Daphne half a dozen times hoping to find the answer in a diaper.

"Here," the doctor said, pointing. "You see this small bump?"

Daphne peered. It wasn't obvious, but she was sure of one thing. "I've never seen that before."

"Probably not, or you'd have heard this scream-ing before. I believe it's a hernia."

She looked up quickly at the doctor, her heart jumping, her stomach fluttering unhappily. "Is that dangerous?"

"Depends, but it's an easy fix. I'm going to get an ultrasound to confirm my suspicion."

But Diane wasn't happy to let it go at that. "Why does it depend?"

The doctor smiled over the squalling baby at her. "If it goes on too long, depending on how large a her-nia it is, it could incarcerate the bowel. That would be a problem. This doesn't appear to be that bad— the bowel sounds were normal, if sluggish. I'm bet-ting this problem is just showing up. But we'll see. In the meantime..."

He pressed on that small bump in Daphne's abdo-men until it was flat. "Gently," he said.

It was as if someone had flipped a switch. Daphne stopped shrieking, instead snuffling and making hic-cuping sounds as she began to settle.

"There you go," the doctor said. "You can hold her, but don't feed her. The ultrasound tech shouldn't be long, but...what I just did is pretty much diagnos-tic. A small incision, some stitches and this girl is going to be just fine."

"But what did you just do?"

"I pushed her intestine back through the hernia. It won't last, unfortunately, but for a little while she can rest."

Diane sank back into the chair, feeling as if some-one had let all the air out of her. The child was going to be okay. One little press and Daphne had become quieter. A couple of stitches inside and she'd be bet-ter. Right?

"We'll talk about the surgery after I look at the ultrasound," the doctor said. "I'll see you again shortly."

Diane wanted only one thing—to hold her little girl again. But she sagged in the chair as if some-one had cut her strings. It fell to Blaine to wrap the baby up in a blanket and place her in Diane's arms.

She looked at him, wishing she could fall into the pools of his blue eyes. They brought good things to mind, like sunny summer skies, so at odds with the moment. "It's going to be all right."

"That's what it sounds like." The corners of his eyes creased as he smiled. "Although I wouldn't be surprised if she starts screaming again before all this is done. A hernia."

"I'm not even sure what that is."

"He'll tell us, I'm sure, but it's my understanding it can be an opening in the intestinal wall. That's why he could push her intestine back in."

Diane tried to absorb that while rocking gently and looking down into Daphne's face. The girl had fallen into exhausted slumber, a relief of huge pro-portions for both her and her daughter.

Her daughter. She realized that was the first time

she had thought of Daphne that way without any qualifiers. Her daughter.

There was a scrape, and she looked around to see that Blaine had pulled another chair into the cubicle. He put it beside hers and sat, reaching over to place his hand on her arm. "How are you managing, Diane?"

"Relieved. Worried." She gave a small, tired laugh. "Is it possible to feel both at the same time? Because I think I do."

"Wouldn't surprise me. Poor little tot, poor little mam. You're both wiped, I'm thinking."

"You can skip the diminutive with me," she told him. "Just because I'm a woman…"

He quickly held up a hand, looking as serious as a judge. "I didn't mean any such thing. Sometimes my tongue slips into old ways."

She nodded and let it go. More important things to worry about, anyway. Daphne needed surgery. The doctor might make it sound minor, but Diane wasn't inclined to think any surgery could be perfectly minor, especially not if it involved anesthesia. Such a tiny person in her arms, utterly vulnerable.

She couldn't sit any longer. Holding Daphne close to her breast, she rose and began to pace the tiny cubicle. She felt as if ants of anxiety crawled all over her. The doctor made it sound so simple, but she was sure nothing involved with surgery was that simple. No way. All kinds of things could go wrong, and she was sure that before they went ahead with an operation, she was going to be handed something to sign, something that warned her of every potential peril involved in what they were about to do.

But what else could she do? She couldn't allow Daphne to keep suffering these bouts of pain, and there was no guarantee that they would remain harmless over time. *Incarcerate* was a word used by the doctor, and her mind threw up all kinds of terrifying possibilities. Whatever it took, she had to try her utmost to get her daughter cured, and creating imagined problems wouldn't help.

She paused her pacing, looking down once again into that small, sweet face, relaxed and sleeping at last. The tyke had to be exhausted, but Diane wasn't doing much better. Helpless. God, she had just faced the worst sense of helplessness in her life. Somehow, she sensed that this little girl was going to give her that feeling more than once over the years ahead.

"It's normal to be nervous," Blaine remarked in his deep, slightly gravelly voice. "Mam nearly lost it when my brother Liam fell off his bike and was coldcocked. Kid was definitely alive, but by the time the docs reassured her, I think we'd held a full wake and were moving onto a memorial."

He was trying to make her laugh, she realized. Lighten her fears. She tried a smile but was sure it didn't reach her eyes. "I'm sorry I'm not handling this better, Blaine. It's minor, right?"

He sprang from his chair to surround her and the baby with his large, powerful arms. "It's not minor.

It'll probably be fixed all right, and things will get better, but it's not minor. Don't you apologize. I'm fairly certain no mother wants to be facing any kind of surgery for her babe."

"But he made it sound so...so..."

"Routine? Maybe it is for him. He's got his hands inside people all the time. For you it's not routine."

His words drew her up, releasing her tension enough for a small bubble of humor to burst out. "His hands inside people all the time?"

"Sure, and what else does a physician do? One end or the other, or with a scalpel, they're inside someone. That may be okay for him, but not so easy on the rest of us."

A small, amused sound escaped her. "You're priceless, Blaine."

"I'm quite sure not many would agree with you."

Another thought struck her. Apparently her mind was slipping back into gear as fear faded a little. "You don't have to hang around here. This could take all day. I feel guilty for taking so much of your time."

"I'll be hearing none of that. Wasn't planning to be anywhere else today except putting some furniture together for Daphne."

At last she was able to settle on the chair again, Daphne snugly in her arms, filling a hole inside her she'd never felt before. "I'm sure you have a life. You've spent a lot of time this week looking after me and Daphne."

"I have a life." He repeated the words as if thinking about them, his face falling into unusually charming lines. "I guess I do. Let me see. It's the weekend, so the county is going to have to wait unless there's a true emergency. So what would I be doing? I might take my horse out for a ride. Or I might settle at my home desk and work on a floor plan for a dream house that I'll probably never like well enough to build."

"Really? Why not?"

"Because I never learned to dream realistically." He flashed a smile. "By the time a house would have everything I could possibly want in it, I'd need to be a very wealthy man, and civil engineers generally don't command that kind of pay. So it's just a dream. But I like it. Right now I'm also thinking about buying a run-down ranch and fixing it up. For my horse, of course. What about you? What do you do with your free time?"

"What free time?" she asked drily. "I think that vanished with Daphne."

"Only for a few months. You'll find it again."

Just then Daphne stirred and made a little sound. Her lips puckered and the tip of her tongue appeared. "She's getting hungry."

"Then I guess she'll be squalling again soon, because the doc said not to feed her. Don't you have a dodie for her?"

"Dodie?"

"Ah…" Blaine hesitated. "Pacifier."

"Oh! It's one of those things I haven't gotten yet. She doesn't seem to look for one."

"Maybe not. It's a soothing thing for babies, but not everyone approves."

"What's to disapprove?"

He shrugged. "People with children can argue about a great many things. Seems like there are a million ways to do things. Don't get overwhelmed by advice. My mother used dodies. Said it saved her mind."

"I can imagine, with that many kids."

"We didn't make life easy for her." He winked. "Nor did we get much easier. Scamps to the last of us. I'm convinced she had a personal relationship with the Blessed Mother because she referred to her all the time. As in, 'Blessed Mother, what were you t'inking, Blaine?'"

A silent laugh escaped Diane as she realized just how glad she was to have him with her. He was keeping her from plunging all the way into the fear that had been gnawing at her since she realized Daphne's crying wasn't mere irritability. Little by little he was pulling her up, steadying her.

Considering how much lay ahead of her still, she was extremely glad he hadn't opted to take off and come back later. At some point she was going to have to turn her precious little bundle over to strangers who would operate on her. She couldn't feel comfortable about that. Just couldn't.

Before she could chase the rabbit of worry any farther, a pretty young woman wheeled in a machine nearly bigger than she was. "Hi, I'm Cassie from ultrasound. I'm just going to take a look at the baby, all right? Her name is Daphne, isn't it?"

"Yes."

The tech nodded, scanning a screen. "Suspected hernia, lower right quadrant. Does that sound correct to you?"

"Yes." Diane felt her nerves tightening up again. Why so many questions?

"Please bring Daphne over here and place her on the bed," Cassie said. "And please unwrap her."

Diane rose, realizing that the boulder was rolling downhill again, that she wasn't going to be able to do anything about any of this except let others care for Daphne.

Her hands shook a little as she began to unwrap the blankets. Daphne woke and made a few irritable cries.

"She's going to be even more angry with me, Mom," Cassie said. "I keep the gel on a warming pad, but I can't make it too warm. She's not going to be happy about this. You just stand on the far side of the bed and hold her hand and left leg. I'd like to minimize wiggling so I can get a clearer view. Dad, you can help, too, if you like."

Part of Diane noted that Blaine had been identified as Daphne's dad and that he didn't object, merely came over to help if he could.

Barely realizing she was doing it, Diane began to coo to Daphne, talking quietly, reassuringly as she sometimes did when she was feeding the girl.

Daphne's eyes darted around then found her face. She leaned in as close as she dared, trying not to get into the tech's way.

Of course, that didn't help much when the cool gel hit Daph's skin, along with the probe.

"Easy there, girl," Cassie said gently, her attention on a screen that was showing a whole bunch of stuff that didn't make any sense to Diane. "Ah," Cassie said on a breath. "I think we've got it. Let me just do a little more…"

Daphne definitely didn't like this. Her cries became angrier, and both Blaine and Diane tried to keep her from squirming too much.

"There we go," said Candy. She pulled a disposable cloth out of a dispenser and wiped away all the gel. "She'll calm in a minute. Even adults don't always like this. You can wrap her up again if you want. The doctor won't be long."

A minute later she trundled out with her machine and Diane heard her say, "Mr. Madden, are you back again? What's that leg up to now?"

Diane reached around for the blanket, but Blaine grabbed it first and wrapped Daphne up snugly. He held her for a minute, looking down into her tiny face, then turned her over to Diane.

"Hard to hand her over," he said gruffly.

"I know. I don't want to let go of her. But I guess I'm going to have to." Then she lifted her gaze from her daughter to him. "I can't begin to tell you how grateful I am. I know she's going to be in good hands, but it helps not to be alone."

"I'm glad to be here," he responded. "But I wish that doc would hurry. Tenterhooks were never designed to be comfortable. My God, these people act as if they have all day."

None of that was very flattering, but Diane could understand his feeling, because she shared it. The intellectual realization that Daphne wasn't the only patient they were dealing with didn't help at all. Selfishly, she wanted her daughter to have everyone's full attention.

Daphne was starting to squirm, her face reddening. "Oh, no," she whispered. "Not again. Hurting like that…" She might scream. She might drown this ER with a volume Diane couldn't match.

Blaine took Daphne and put her on his shoulder, patting her back rather firmly.

"What are you doing?" she asked.

"Damned if I know. Maybe a change of position will keep things from getting worse. Hell, maybe I should dangle her by her ankles so all the pressure goes in the other direction."

"I heard that." Into the room walked the doctor. "Sorry for the wait. Let me call up those sonogram results and show you what I can. Daphne will be going to surgery in about thirty minutes, as soon as the surgeon is done with his current patient. You need to relax, Mom. This isn't life-threatening, even though it's miserable for her."

"You're sure about that?" Diane said almost defiantly. She was beginning to feel as if she was caught in a nightmare without end. She tried to tell herself she was being ridiculous, but the feeling persisted. She wanted a speed that a hospital couldn't possibly provide to someone who wasn't dying then and there.

Blaine slipped his free arm around her shoulders. He gave her a gentle squeeze.

"Okay," said the doctor, pulling up an image. "Without a practiced eye, it's hard to see, but about two inches of her intestinal wall haven't grown together. That's actually not a terribly unusual thing, although we more often see it in boys. Anyway, nothing abnormal, and I'm glad to tell you we can take care of this immediately. There's absolutely no reason to wait. She'll be going home with you late this afternoon once she recovers from the anesthesia."

Hope leaped in Diane's heart. "Today?"

The doctor smiled. "Today. Really. Now, what's going to happen next is we're going to have to start an IV. That's usually the first thing we do when someone is to be admitted, but I didn't want to do that until we were certain what we were dealing with and when we'd deal with it. Of course, if I'd seen any sign of dehydration..." He shrugged. "We're going to put it in her forehead."

Diane froze. She felt Blaine stiffen beside her.

"What do you mean?" Diane demanded.

"The best way to give a child this small an IV is to place it in a scalp vein." He leaned over and touched

Daphne high on her forehead. "About here." Daphne made an irritated sound and tried to suck her fist.

"Why there?" The idea horrified Diane.

"Because it's the best, easiest and safest place for a child this young. I promise you, you don't want us trying to find a vein in a waving arm or leg, especially not through the layer of baby fat. We can do this in a minute. Anywhere else and we're going to have to restrain her and look hard. Looking for a good IV site is sometimes…"

"Painful," Blaine finished. "Watched it with my mother when she had trouble birthing Leanna. I swear, the woman doesn't have any veins."

The doctor smiled faintly. "I've run into folks like that. Anyway, Mom, trust me. This won't bother Daphne, and it's only for a few hours, anyway. But I'm going to ask you to leave her with the nurses, because you're not going to want to watch it."

Diane didn't need a diagram. Ten minutes later she'd been banished to a waiting room with Blaine, and her heart and arms felt empty.

"He sounds so…cavalier."

Blaine shook his head. "He's not. He's just used to this in a way we aren't. For him it's all in a day's work. At least he was sensitive about explaining where the IV has to go and why."

Blaine took her hand and held it snugly. A miracle of a man, she thought. Anyone else would probably have fled from this situation. Not even remotely was it his problem.

"I'm so glad I met you," she told him honestly. "I'd have been so lost without you, and you're so…so stalwart. A lot of guys would have headed for the hills."

"Stalwart, huh?" he said with a devilish smile. "I'm liking that. Also, just so you know, I'm not one to run for the hills. Mam tried to raise me with some sense, but I get all stubborn-like sometimes. Just so ya know," he repeated. Then his grin faded a bit. "I'm not unique, Diane. I learned that a long time ago."

"Who would have told you that?" It was a question that didn't expect an answer. Of course no one would have said such a thing to him. But to her dismay, he *did* answer.

"Apart from getting knocked upside the head for being so full of myself, you mean?" His smile faded even more. "No joke. Her name was Ailis."

"Ailish?" She tried to repeat it but wasn't sure she said it correctly.

"Call her Alice. My first big nosedive into a heap called love."

She felt her heart squeeze for him. That amused her briefly, but her thoughts darted right back to Daphne. This shouldn't take long, she assured herself. The doctor had made it sound like a quick nip and tuck. Trying to distract herself, she said absently, "Sometimes you don't sound like you come from Ireland. Is that on purpose?"

"Some of it. I need to be understood, and a good, thick Galway accent might get in the way. But most of us grew up speaking English, Diane. Even if not the queen's own English."

"No Gaelic?"

"Irish Gaelic is something we have to make a special effort to learn. Some is being taught in school now, but what's the point in a country where everyone speaks English?"

She nodded, taking it in. "It seems a shame."

"Seven hundred years of a shame," he replied.

Mary appeared in the door of the small waiting room. "We're taking Daphne to surgery now," she said. "I'll come get you as soon as she's in recovery."

Diane leaped to her feet. "How long?"

Mary smiled. "I can't say exactly. This shouldn't be time-consuming. Why don't you go to the cafeteria and get a light meal? You'll hardly have time to eat it."

"That sounded reassuring," Diane remarked as she watched Mary disappear. She reached out blindly and found Blaine's hand. "They keep calling me Mom."

"Well, you are the gal's mom. It hardly needs the adjective *foster*, if you ask me." He turned toward her. "From what you said, you may be the only mother the child ever has. Now let's go check out the cafeteria. You need something in your stomach, and I know I do. Hell, I even left the coffees in the car. I wasn't worrying much, was I?"

"But you seemed so calm," she objected as they strode toward the cafeteria.

"Rule," he said. "Only one person allowed to panic at a time."

"I like that rule," she agreed, her heart lightening a bit. Daphne was heading into surgery. The doctor had said it was minor. In theory she should get her baby back with nothing but a small scar and a couple of stitches, and then Daphne would never have this pain again. That was a good thing, however rough these hours had been, including the ones looming ahead of her.

The cafeteria wasn't terribly busy. A few people, looking as if they had someone in the hospital, sat at some of the small tables. A few people in scrubs occupied others. It wasn't a large cafeteria, but the selection was good. Evidently they had passed breakfast at some point and were now on to lunch. Sandwiches dominated the offerings.

Diane selected a ham and swiss on rye with a small salad. Blaine chose roast beef on a hard roll— two of them, actually. Apparently he had a large appetite. They had no trouble finding a table to themselves, and Blaine left her for a few minutes to return with coffee.

"The tea was out of an urn. I can't vouch for it," he said as he put a paper cup in front of her. "Of course, I can't vouch for the coffee, either."

"All I'm going to say is thank you." She closed her eyes for a few minutes, head tilted forward, as she tried to release the tension in her neck. God, it was going to take more than a hot bath to wash away this tightness. Time had truly developed leaden feet, and the first thing she did when she opened her eyes was seek a clock.

Time seemed to be as much a secret in a hospital cafeteria as the average department store. She thought about pulling out her cell phone, then decided against it. She had no idea how long this would take, so why count minutes?

"Eat," Blaine prodded kindly. "You won't be much help to the daffodil if you need a bed beside her."

Obediently she picked up her sandwich. Blaine was already halfway through his first. "Why do you call her daffodil?"

"It's better than Daffy?"

She'd forgotten she'd asked that question before, but against all reason, that dragged a laugh out of her. "I guess so." At last she bit into her sandwich, enjoying the crunch of fresh lettuce and the beautifully melding flavors of ham and cheese. Dang, she hadn't even realized how hungry she was, but as her mouth tasted sustenance, her stomach grumbled to remind her she hadn't eaten since dinner last night.

Then she remembered something. "Who was Alice?"

He stopped with his second sandwich halfway to his mouth. "Now why would you be wanting to know about her?"

She flushed faintly. "Curiosity, I guess. You mentioned her."

"I did." He took another bite of sandwich.

"I gather she made you feel bad."

"I believe I explained it was my dive into the questionable nightmare called love."

She couldn't help it. A little giggle escaped her. "A flattering description of romance."

"Did I say it was a romance? Blessed Mary, it was no such thing. It didn't get that far."

"Oh." She chewed and thought. "Then what was it?"

He sighed, took a long draft of his coffee or tea and put down the second half of his sandwich. "I'm not in the way of discussing such things."

"You struck out, then."

"Ack." He regarded her, his blue eyes intense but a hint of amusement around his mouth nonetheless. "Ailis can only be explained by my callow youth. And only my callow youth could have caused me to be such a nuisance. She hardly saw me, and when she did she slapped me back into my place. 'Blaine Harrigan,' she said, 'I've got better things to do with me time than be annoyed by the likes of you.' Quite clear, I thought, but I'd been enough of a fool that my friends had a great time teasing me."

He spoke lightly about it, but she wasn't sure she could accept that. After all, he'd mentioned in the first place, bringing it up when denying he was in any way unique. This Ailis or Alice must have cut him hard.

"She could have been kinder."

He shook his head, and now the smile was unmistakable. "I told you I'm stubborn. I should have taken the hints."

But the few minutes of calm and normalcy began to desert her. She needed to get back to the other side of the hospital; she needed to know what was happening with Daphne. Some word. Any word.

Blaine evidently sensed it when she dropped her sandwich and stirred.

"Let's go," he said, rising. "Shall I bring that coffee for you?"

"Please."

Damn, she was yo-yoing, something she wasn't at all used to. She'd lived a reasonably calm life, focused around her job and a few friends to have a good time with on weekends. The only person who'd ever brought her close to this kind of up-and-downing was Max, and he didn't hold a candle to Daphne.

Right alongside her worry for the girl, an amazement was beginning to grow. One week and she'd given her heart to Daphne, apparently. Man, she'd thought it would take longer than that.

But maybe there was something special about infants. Maybe they just naturally brought out maternal instincts. Although, she thought wryly, until recently she hadn't thought she had any.

Evidently, she did now.

Chapter Six

An eternity seemed to have passed before Mary came to find them. "She's out of surgery," the nurse told them cheerfully. "We'll give her some time to wake up and then you can see her, all right?"

Blaine looked at Diane and thought the woman looked like she'd been through the wringer. She'd hung on to her emotions really well, but the worry and stress had just about used up her reserves.

Hardly surprising. His own mother had looked like a scarecrow by the time Liam had wakened from his concussion. Nothing like the investment of a mother, he thought.

About five minutes later, they received what probably qualified as one of the most important visits of the day. A doctor walked in, not the one they'd seen in the emergency room, and sat in a chair facing them.

"Daphne's parents, right?"

Blaine didn't answer but Diane merely nodded.

"I'm Dr. Howe. I performed the surgery on your daughter. It was uncomplicated and she's just fine. The nurse is going to give you some treatment orders you'll need to follow for a week, but she's young and healthy and Daphne will be perfectly well in no time at all. We gave her some antibiotics through the IV to prevent any possible infection, but you're going to have to stay up with it at home." He looked to each of them, awaiting a nod.

Only then did he smile. "For what it's worth, I wish it were this easy to fix everything. Your little girl won't have any problems, and maybe best of all, she won't remember this."

"But I will," Diane murmured, barely aware she spoke aloud.

"Yes, you will," the doctor answered. "Dad? I think Mom needs a little nap when she gets home, don't you?"

"Absolutely."

"We'll be releasing Daphne shortly. She's waking, and she didn't need much anesthesia at all. She'll be kicking and cooing by the time you get her."

What a lovely picture he painted, Diane thought. Then without warning, Blaine wrapped her in his arms and held her close, her head on his shoulder.

"You can relax now," he said quietly. "I've even been told I'm a grand babysitter."

Somehow she didn't doubt that at all.

Blaine took over because it seemed right to him. Diane had been through a wringer, however good the outcome. He hadn't, simply because he hadn't made the same kind of emotional investment in the baby yet. Plus, he hadn't been wakened to screeching that had to have been terrifying to someone who'd never heard it before.

Diane dozed on his shoulder and he held her comfortably, hoping it would both rejuvenate her and make the time pass more rapidly. Whatever these medical people meant by "shortly" took quite a bit longer than that. The clock on the waiting room wall seemed to be keeping good time, and it told him that this had probably lasted as long as it had felt. Midafternoon was creeping up on them and the baby still hadn't been released.

But at last it happened and they were taking her home. The nurse, Mary, had advised them that Daphne might not be hungry or thirsty for a while. The IV would have met her needs for liquid and sugar, plus she'd probably be tired enough after all this to just want to sleep.

Blaine eyed the small white bandage on her forehead where the needle had evidently been inserted and murmured, "Poor girl," as he placed her in the playpen, the easiest place for her to move about if she wanted. Plus, Diane could keep an eye on her from the comfort of her recliner.

Diane looked pooped enough to need that nap that had been suggested, but she seemed fixated on Daphne, as if she were afraid the girl might stop breathing. Not knowing what else to do, Blaine brought her one of the sticky buns he'd bought hours ago and handed her the small plate.

"I just had a sandwich," she reminded him.

"Half of one, as I recall, and not as recently as you think. It's been a busy long day. Calories, woman. Calories."

"What time is it, anyway?"

"The afternoon is mostly gone."

Diane stiffened. "It seemed like a long time, but that long?"

"Daffodil here was getting the best care," he reminded her. "They didn't want you popping out the door with her only to come running back in because she was bleeding or something. The recovery room probably took longer than either of us noticed."

All of a sudden he wished he could look another direction. She'd slept with his arm around her for longer than she knew, and the experience had provoked him with simmering heat. It had also distracted him from noting just how long they'd waited. He wished he could drag his gaze away from her for fear of what it might reveal. If eyes could speak, his were probably shouting. Wrong time. Maybe never. *Get a grip, Blaine.*

* * *

She looked at him, into his deep blue eyes, trying to pull her scattered and scattering thoughts together. "How…"

"Well, you may not remember, but you dozed on my shoulder for a long while." He made it sound light, simple. Not as sexual as she'd found it, despite all that was going on. In fact, some of her reactions to being held by him had felt crass to her. Maybe just a form of denial?

She lifted a hand to her mouth. "Oh, Blaine, I'm so sorry."

He waved away her apology. "No need. I'm not complaining. I was glad to see you get a little sleep, though I doubt it was restful. You still look like you could use more of it, too, so nap if you like."

She shook her head, suddenly feeling very, very sad. "I'm taking over your life. I never meant to do that."

"I haven't resisted, either, and I'm perfectly capable of saying no. I seem to remember inserting myself last night and this morning. Besides, what's a little help with a sick baby and some furniture assembly? Any neighbor would help with either. Now relax."

"How can I when I feel guilty?"

"Guilty?" He dropped to the floor, sitting cross-legged.

"I need to get you a decent chair," she remarked, but she'd averted her gaze.

"Forget the chair. I've sat on harder ground and with six kids we often didn't have enough chairs. So what's making you feel guilty?"

"Everything," she said extravagantly, waving her hand. The strange sadness that had crept up on her was probably making her as stupid as the fatigue she was feeling.

"That's a whole lot," he said when she didn't continue.

"Well, look at me. I came out here to take a new job, just figuring that somehow everything was going to fall into place. I know damn all about caring for an infant, I still haven't found a good day care for her, partly because I've been too busy to really look, so that's hanging out at the courthouse. Then she gets sick and I don't even know what to do about it. I'm a big failure, and I can't imagine what I would have done if you hadn't showed up this morning."

"Ah." He leaned back, bracing himself on his hands. "Let me reiterate. You quite naturally accepted a job you wanted, right?"

"I shouldn't have."

"I think you're getting the sequence a bit out of step here. You accepted the job."

She nodded, getting the feeling that he was about to make her feel even more inadequate, and after today, she was quite certain she deserved it.

"Anybody would have accepted a job they wanted. What else got me all the way out here so far from me home that I can't even talk right?"

Damn, he was going to make her laugh. She didn't want to laugh. She'd made a whole bunch of screwups in just a week. She kept her eyes closed for fear that if she looked at Blaine right now she'd probably jump into his arms for comfort. Comfort from what? Everything had turned out all right with Daphne, hadn't it?

"I see the corner of your mouth twitching. It's not sacrilege to laugh. As events happened, you must have quit your old job when you accepted the new, unless you're more of a scamp that I would believe. Like anyone else, you were getting ready to come out here for this one when, all unexpectedly, your cousin's baby needed you. Instead of simply saying no and leaving the child to be a ward of the state, you took on an unexpected responsibility."

She couldn't exactly argue that, although it wasn't looking so very smart right now. She wasn't even a good caretaker for Daphne. That much had become abundantly clear this morning.

"Now you have your hands full while starting a new job in a way you were utterly unprepared for. I think I told you, most people have nine months to get ready. How many days did you have?"

She sighed, clenching her hands, and admitting it. "Only a week, because I was leaving, and then she was in my care for only a couple of days before I got here—which made it even more stupid."

"Not stupid. You needed to keep this job, now more than ever because you had an extra person to care for. Thus, here you are. Since I see a living, breathing baby in the playpen over there, just what exactly did you mess up?"

She bit her lip, fighting back that inexplicable sorrow that kept trying to wash over her. At last she looked at Blaine. "I don't have day care, for one thing. The board isn't going to tolerate this forever. And I didn't know what I should do this morning! If you hadn't come over…"

"If I hadn't barged my way in, you'd eventually have reached the same conclusion—Daphne needed a doctor, and the only place to get one on Saturday morning is an emergency room."

"You can't be sure…"

"I can be quite sure," he said firmly, "that you're not the unkind, uncaring sort of person who would have let that child cry for much longer."

She sat up straighter, looking at her daughter. *Her daughter.* The realization settled in her heart for the second time that day. She was now Daphne's mother. For real. And she knew next to nothing about what this child needed.

"I'm scared," she said quietly.

"About what?"

"She's my daughter. Blaine, it just hit me today."

He scooted closer and rested his hand on her knee. The touch was comforting, warm. "What did?"

"That this isn't some temporary thing. I mean…I know my cousin will probably never be well enough to care for Daphne. That's why they hunted me up.

She'd already spent a month in the care of social services, and they hoped I'd take her rather than an unrelated foster family."

"Which you did."

She shook her head a little. "I don't think... Something about today made me truly realize that this isn't temporary. That she's mine now. My *daughter*."

He tilted his head to one side and squeezed her knee gently. "This is somehow more terrifying? I seem to have come into the middle of the conversation."

"It's more terrifying," she said truthfully. "This isn't some temporary thing I'm dealing with for a few months or a year. I think I was deluding myself at first, believing that MaryJo would get better. Only from what the social worker said, MaryJo is never going to get well enough to care for a child. Why did that not penetrate before?"

"I'm not sure what you mean by penetrate. You already told me how sick your cousin is, and that she'd never be a mother to this child."

"I know. It was all laid out. I knew. I just didn't *know*, if that makes any sense."

"Ah," he said in his deep rumble of a voice. "It was real to the head but not yet to the heart?"

She nodded slowly and raised a hand to massage the tension growing in her neck. "I think that's probably a good way to put it. But it sounds stupid. All day today I've been thinking how inadequate I am to this, how I should have thought more clearly rather than acting instinctively about Daphne. What kind of mother will I be? I never even babysat!"

He raised his knee, resting his arm on it. She wished the movement hadn't taken his hand away, because it had been so comforting. She didn't even bother to try to talk herself out of the feeling. Today was a mess of feelings and fears.

"While today may have seemed to prove me a total liar," he said, "the truth still is that caring for a baby is easy."

"Like I'm going to believe that now?" Indeed, her mind was running around like a skittering mouse, imagining or trying to imagine a million other bad things that could happen to Daphne. The world suddenly seemed full of threats, and that baby was utterly dependent on her to deal with them.

"It's easy," Blaine repeated firmly. "Think about it, woman. You've been caring for her for over a week now and she doesn't look any worse for the wear."

"Until this morning."

He snorted and uttered a word that she was quite sure didn't qualify as polite even in his home country. "Listen to me, Diane. I mostly raised four of the six me mam had, and if I couldn't break 'em, you can't, either. What happened today was *not* the result of anything you did or didn't do. Gad, babies are only half-baked, ya know. It's not unusual to find some little thing that hasn't finished growing. Most of 'em take care of themselves, but every now and then this happens. Me younger sister, Bridey, was born tongue-tied."

The surprised Diane right out of her preoccupation with imagined horrors. "What's that?"

He curved up one corner of his mouth. "Given how much the gal talks, it might have been better to leave her that way. Naw, it just meant that her tongue was still attached to the bottom of her mouth. After a little cut it's all better. It's the same for the daffodil over there."

Diane desperately hoped he was right. She looked over at Daphne. "Shouldn't she be waking by now? She certainly must need a diaper change."

He rose in one fluid movement then lifted the sleepy baby into Daphne's arms. "You take care of that, Mama. I'm in the way of heading over to the diner to get us a dinner."

"You don't have to stay," she said impulsively, although she was very glad of his company.

His eyes creased at the corners as he smiled, then he winked. "I figured that out. I'll be back."

She looked down at the drowsy bundle in her arms and hoped he meant that.

Blaine left the car behind and walked the three blocks to the diner. The evening air was cool and pleasant, the twilight just beginning to deepen. Kids played outside, waiting to be called to dinner, their voices cheery on the gentle breeze.

He figured after the day's stress, Diane would

probably be glad of some one-on-one time with Daphne. Quiet time to regain her footing. A chance to follow the postoperative directions for wound care without someone breathing over her shoulder. Tonight wouldn't be difficult, anyway. They'd placed a waterproof bandage over the incision and had given Diane a few more and some antibacterial swabs to use if the bandage got loose.

Other than that, they seemed to think the kid would pretty much be good to go by tomorrow. No special treatment required. Return for follow up with the surgeon on Monday.

In all, neither of them could have asked for a better outcome. And now that he was by himself, Blaine was fully willing to admit that most of the confidence he'd displayed this morning had come from the need to keep Diane calmer. She was frantic with worry. He hadn't been doing much better. He'd held a lot of babies over the years, and he could tell when there was serious pain involved. That cry was a class unto itself.

But now that Daphne was on the road to recovery, he started thinking more about Diane. There'd been a refrain wandering through the things she'd been saying, and it was becoming clearer to him.

He wondered what the hell had savaged her self-confidence. The woman had an advanced degree in urban planning. From what he'd heard in casual conversation with the commissioners since he'd learned of her hiring, she could have easily chosen a job in a much bigger city, or with a huge developer. Instead she had chosen to come here because she wanted to try out her ideas and run the show.

Understandable. Courageous, even, because if she messed up, there'd be no one else to blame. It would all fall on her.

But how often, today alone, had he heard her self-doubt? He was quite sure he'd heard her talk about failing more than once.

Someone must have done that to her, because her accomplishments hadn't included failures he'd heard about. Not from the commissioners who'd hired her, not from her résumé, not from her letters of reference. Perhaps she was only confident when it came to her work, and not outside it.

Not that he could imagine any reason for that. She was a beautiful woman who could stir a man just by breathing. Or at least could stir him. He'd have to be careful he didn't let that show, because Diane had quite enough on her plate right now.

The walk to the diner wasn't a long one, but he walked slowly. Usually he was accustomed to striding swiftly, but tonight he wanted to give Diane that little bit of time. Maybe she'd want him to leave as soon as he brought dinner. He couldn't blame her.

Today had been stressful for hours, sitting in that hospital waiting for her child to be returned, wondering what was going on, the fear before the diagnosis… all of it added up to a rough day.

Especially for a woman who had just invited a child fully into her heart.

That struck him—her explanation how today the reality had come home. This was no longer a temporary gig, but a permanent one, and the responsibility seemed to be overwhelming her.

Well, if she'd let him, he'd be glad to help a bit with that. While he'd sometimes resented it when he was younger, now he was glad that so much had been expected of him in the way of taking care of young'uns.

Like any youngster, he'd wished for more time to spend with his mates. But when he'd picked up Daphne for the first time on Monday, he'd realized how very much he had missed caring for his siblings.

Just goes to show, he thought. You never knew what you had until it was gone.

Then he was facing the diner and could delay no longer. He had a hankering for a piece of Maude's fine apple pie, but that wouldn't suffice. Diane needed a decent meal.

He stood outside the door, reading the menu taped to the window, trying to find something different but nutritious. The default steak sandwich that everyone around here loved so much might be too heavy after the day she'd had. He could still remember his mother preferring light meals after an upsetting day.

Diane could be different, but he didn't want to find out the hard way. Eventually he settled on some homemade chicken soup and a stack of Texas toast. If that didn't do, he'd come back for something else.

As he'd been standing there, people coming and going had greeted him. It was a nice feeling to be known by so many, and he hoped Diane would soon enjoy it. In the meantime, he headed inside to place his order and discovered everyone already knew what had happened to Daphne.

Who the hell at the hospital had talked, he wondered, but with amusement. It could have been a janitor. They might not be covered by HIPAA rules. What did he know? Hard to keep a secret in this town, anyway.

Maude gave him a bucket of soup big enough for an army, added a huge stack of toast and threw in several pieces of pie.

"You know the way to my heart, woman."

She sniffed. "It's the way to every man's heart."

But he caught a glimmer of humor in her usually harsh expression. He wondered if the heart attack a few months back had softened her up some. Gad, if that were true, nobody in this town would be sure she was Maude.

Amused, he stepped outside with two plastic bags of goodies and resolved to make a nice pot of tea when he got back to the house.

He passed others out to enjoy the pleasant evening. Five years here and he was still getting used to the different seasons. It was his Galway upbringing. He liked to say that his home had two seasons:

wet and chilly or wetter and chillier. Which wasn't fair to the old country, because they had some glorious days when the sun broke through the familiar overcast and painted the land in shades of gold and green. At times, when the north wind blew, they even saw a bit of snow.

Still, it was a good joke.

When he reached Diane's little house, he let himself in quietly, unsure whether she and the baby might have fallen asleep.

Indeed they had. Diane was curled in her battered old recliner with Daphne snuggled in her arm and a blanket over them.

All was well in the Finch world. Smiling, he went to the kitchen and started the kettle. He needed some tea, but the soup would be easy to heat later.

Then he settled at the kitchen table and waited, much as he would have liked to just sit and watch mother and child sleep. So peaceful after a day that had been anything but.

Eventually he heard fussy sounds emanating from the living room. Daphne was returning to the world and probably wanted food and a diaper change. He should leave that to Diane, he decided. He absolutely didn't want her to think he was taking over, and he might have given her that sense more than once.

But he was definitely bothered by her feeling like a failure. He'd like to explore the reasons for that if the time ever came. Right now, even after today, they were still just acquaintances. Blaine was of a type to just walk into the middle of a relationship of any kind, and hadn't his mam warned him about that? Often as it was, he didn't suffer much trouble for it, but he wound up with a lot of friends. There still always remained a possibility that he'd be told to scat, the way Ailis had. He'd learned to take his knocks over time, but he sincerely hoped Diane wouldn't send him on his way. He was growing fond of that woman.

A few minutes later, she came to the kitchen with Daphne freshly changed into a new jumper and sucking on her fist as her bright eyes looked around.

"Hey," Diane said. "I need to open a can of formula. Would you mind?"

Clearly she didn't want to let go of the babe after today. He had no problem with that. "Where do I find it?"

She pointed. "In that pantry. The clean nursing bottles are on the shelf beside it."

And there they were, all sparkly clean and carefully capped. "Should I warm it for her?" He'd always warmed bottles when he was taking care of a newborn sibling, but he'd gathered that didn't always happen.

"Poor thing has been taking it at whatever temperature it comes," Diane answered. "No way to heat it at the office. Tonight, though, let's spoil her. It should heat well enough if you set it in a pan of hot water from the tap."

It certainly would. He'd done it before. Plus, it wasn't that cold in this house. Though some folks would think it too early in the season to be turning on the heat, Diane must not agree. He'd heard the hot air turn on several times.

Diane remained at the kitchen table while she nursed Daphne. She'd agreed a cup of tea sounded good, as did the chicken soup.

"A gallon, I swear," Blaine told her. "I sure hope you like it. Maude really loaded me up."

"I love it." But all her attention was on Daphne, as it should be. Totally absorbed in her new daughter. A grand thing, a mother's love.

The soup hadn't cooled much, but he put some in a pan anyway to warm it slowly. The Texas toast would be on the soggy side, but it always tasted good, anyway. Then he waved some pie under her nose. "A feast awaits."

At last, for the first time that day, she truly smiled. Good, she was getting past the shock of it all. It might hit her again later, but when all was said and done, as emergencies went, this one had been benign.

Not everything could be fixed so easily.

He placed a cup of tea and a plate with a wedge of thick toast on it in front of her. He figured if she wanted to, she could hold that bottle with one hand and eat with the other. A necessary maternal skill since the powers that be hadn't granted a mother a third arm.

When Daphne had finished about half of her bottle, now trying to hold it with her tiny hands although she couldn't yet, Diane propped it with the blanket and took a few sips of her tea.

"Delicious," she announced.

"Steeped longer," he answered. "No secret. Our daffodil looks content with the world."

Diane nodded. "Strangely enough, as far as she's concerned, nothing happened."

"Great advantage of an infant's memory."

She laughed softly. "I wish mine worked like that sometimes." She looked up from the baby at him. "Did you get your culvert problem sorted out?"

She'd already asked him twice, but he allowed it to pass because of the fatiguing, upsetting day. "Well, we've made a start on it. We're going to have to dig out the paving, pull out the deteriorating culvert and start all over again, basically."

She nodded. "Nothing to save?"

"Not now. Between a dozen winters and the heavy rains we had last month, it's pretty much collapsed."

"And that historic storefront you looked at?"

"Well, we had a word or two. Seems the owner and I have a different idea of preservation."

That grabbed her attention. "Now you're talking to my hobbyhorse. Does this town have an historic overlay district?"

"You might say it does. Partially. And that's where we got to disagreeing. Evidently his building isn't on the overlay from when it was made years ago and, in my opinion, it seriously ought to be. We'll need you to take a look, but I extracted his solemn promise on the grounds that if he moves ahead without prior approval, he might have to undo everything."

"Nobody wants that," she said. Daphne had stopped sucking on her bottle and was looking drowsy again. In a movement that felt more natural every day, she placed the child on her shoulder and began to gently pat her back.

"So historic districts are your thing?" he asked.

"Most definitely. Part of what I was told when I interviewed was that the city council wanted more of the town to fall under the protections than it currently does. I wasn't certain at the time what they meant, but it's a job I'd love to take on. It doesn't have to be onerous on the property owners, but evidently there's an appearance some in this town want to preserve."

"I'd call it early-twentieth-century Wild West," he remarked drily. "But I can only say that mostly from movies. Most of this place doesn't resemble that, but it comes from that era. I get the feeling people who came here and settled this town were trying to bring their old homes with them."

"It's entirely likely. I noticed the church with the steeple. New England. Same with the courthouse square, right down to the statue."

He smiled faintly. "The statue of a soldier representing a war no one can identify for certain. This area wasn't settled during the Civil War, as I understand it. That came later." He paused. "Meaning no offense here, but this place might do well to honor some of its Native heritage. I'm sure they were here before the late arrivals."

"I'm sure, and I'm not offended. The city fathers might have a different opinion."

"Don't they always?"

She shifted Daphne from her shoulder to her arm, and the little girl barely stirred. "Time for a diaper change and some sleep, I think."

"Do you want me to take off?"

Her eyes widened. "Why would I want that? Man, Blaine, we haven't even eaten the supper you brought. I just need a minute to put her down."

Apparently, he'd wended the thickets safely enough today, he thought, rising to check on the soup and hunt up some dishes. Selfishly, he wished she weren't so preoccupied with Daphne. He'd kind of like for her to be preoccupied with him in that way.

Not likely and probably not wise. Ah, hell. A randy Irishman, a woman who was in the way of being his boss, if not exactly, and a baby that needed all the attention available.

He ought to be used to that by now. Years of experience and all that.

Besides, and perhaps most important, there was something precious and nearly sacred about a woman with an infant in her arms. Bury the attraction. It had no place here and now.

Chapter Seven

By the following weekend, Diane had begun to feel more settled in every way. She had a routine going with Daphne that seemed to suit them both, and Aubrey's sister-in-law had found a space for Daphne in the infant section of her early-learning school. Daphne seemed to be thriving there so far, and where she hadn't previously been a frequent smiler, she seemed to be smiling most of her waking moments now. When Diane when to pick her up at the end of a workday, she was always greeted with a happy shriek and a huge smile. Surely she wasn't imagining that those arms had begun to reach for *her*?

Added to that was the new pediatrician's approval of Daphne's overall condition. The surgery was healing nicely and rapidly, her weight was good for her length—that had made Diane giggle a bit—and all was good. She had begun to roll herself from side to side, she could lift and hold her head up longer now when she was on her tummy and...

Diane drew a deep breath as she realized just how fast Daphne was making strides in her development. Now that she worried less about her ability to take care of the girl, maybe she should expend a little energy on enjoying her milestones.

And start taking some photos.

Her cell phone rang as she was putting Daph into her car seat at the end of the workday on Friday. It was Blaine. She'd hardly seen him all week. He'd been out and about, and she'd been practicing a form of archaeology on the old development plan, the most recent—it was ancient—historical overlay and speaking with her new bosses about their vision for Conard City and the county.

She spoke to them individually, in a way that wouldn't violate public meeting rules, just to find out if they had some sort of vision they wanted her to pursue.

Of course they did. In their varied ways, they wanted entirely more than was possible. Well, that was better than wanting to keep everything the same. But a number of years ago, a ski resort had made an attempt to build up on the mountain, and part of their plan had been to refurbish the town, to give it a more "Western" look.

Which had left them with the Victorian additions

of brick sidewalks on some of the streets and some pretty fancy lampposts that might have looked good in London nearly two centuries ago. Attractive but touristy.

Properties that were registered as historic had to meet a whole bunch of preservation requirements. What Diane wanted to know was how far they wanted to go with that historic overlay, because right now the old one had been overridden quite a bit.

Her head was all awhirl with the thoughts she'd gathered, and when she at last had Daphne belted into her car seat, she had to call Blaine back.

"Sorry I missed you," she said. "I was putting Daphne in the car. How was your week, and am I wading into some kind of trouble you've heard about?" Because the feedback she was getting wasn't tremendously helpful.

He laughed. "I'm sure you've dealt with self-interested government members before. We'll talk if you have some time this evening. I never got around to putting the crib together after that struggle with the changing table…"

She laughed as she closed the back door and opened the driver's door. "We should have known we were headed for trouble when the box was labeled *Please do not upside down box.*"

"Somebody certainly needed a better translator," he agreed.

She slipped into the driver's seat and poked her key into the ignition. "And you build things all the time. Okay, I'd love for you to come over. I've got to go, because I'm about to drive."

"Fair enough. Dinner from Maude's, or do you want pizza from the place on the edge of town?"

"Pizza actually sounds good."

"I hope it is."

She laughed again and said goodbye. Life here was becoming familiar—she'd dared to take Daphne out to lunch with some of the women from the clerk's office, and all in all, after a little more than two weeks here, she was beginning to feel comfortable.

Except for her job. It was so obvious that the council and commission members who constituted the planning board hadn't bothered to reach an agreement of any kind. This was going to be fun.

She had time when she got home to change Daphne into a fresh diaper and clothes. Ordinarily she bathed her in the evening, but tonight she decided to leave it for morning. The house felt a little chilly to her, and she wandered down the hall with Daphne in her arms to look at the thermostat. Sixty-eight, so the heat was working. Maybe she was the one who was chilled.

Once she'd prepared Daphne's bottle, she settled into what had become her favorite chore—feeding her daughter.

She still hadn't done anything about finding another chair for the living room, she thought as she cuddled Daphne close and smiled into her alert, bright eyes. She was in no condition to invite anyone over, like her new friends at the courthouse and the judge's wife, Amber. Regardless, Blaine ought to have a better seat than the floor, especially with all he'd done for her.

Putting that changing table together had been quite an experience. At one point she'd turned the directions upside down to see if they made more sense. The diagrams, which should have crossed any language barrier at all, had some big blanks.

She'd learned something, though. Blaine had a massive vocabulary of cusswords in what sounded like two languages.

"Pardon me," he'd said at one point, "but cursin' lubricates the brain cells."

She had laughed and still wanted to laugh as she remembered it. For all his cussing, he'd never once expressed frustration in any physical way, but he sure gave his language a workout. It had been quite a show.

He'd managed to put the entire changing table, drawers and all, together in a remarkably short time, considering that the directions were so useless he'd practically had to figure out how to build it himself.

"I should have used the county shop and made you one myself," he said at one point.

"Tsk, using county property for a personal project?" she'd teased. "I think we'd both be in hot water."

"As if this lot care," he muttered in response.

But that had been last weekend, and now that

she'd had a week to get to know her bosses better, her opinion hadn't improved a whole lot. They were politicians, most of them not really very good at it, and all of them more interested in their day jobs. In short, she thought all of them owned businesses and most of their attention was on ways to improve that. Too much, maybe. She didn't know yet.

Blaine arrived just as she was gently pacing with Daphne, encouraging her to expel any gas. The child seemed far more interested in waving her hand and staring at it than burping.

"My, she's growing active," Blaine said as he paused to drop a kiss on the fuzzy little head before going to the kitchen with the pizza box. "I forgot to ask what toppings you like, so I took a wild guess. Lots of veggies and some pepperoni. Okay?"

"Sounds great." And it did. Already the aroma was making her mouth water. "Thank you."

"My pleasure. So how's the tot been doing this week? I've hardly seen you."

"She's in the learning center now, and she seems happy with it. As for me, I've been picking the brains of the members of the planning board."

"Ah." He turned with a smile and reached for Daphne. "May I? So do you need brain bleach after talking with that crew?"

"Not quite," she managed to laugh. "Let's get to that in a minute."

She passed Daphne to him, enjoying the way he held her daughter. She didn't know why, but it still surprised her that a guy would be interested in a baby that wasn't his own. It was usually women who went gaga over infants. Holding Daphne on his shoulder, he rocked gently from side to side. She was still waving her arm, but she didn't seem disturbed by the change of venue.

"The doc said she's doing well?"

"In every respect," she answered, feeling proud for no discernible reason. She hadn't created the child—all she had done was be her caretaker for a few weeks.

"Well, then, clearly you've been managing motherhood just fine, despite your concerns. Grab some of that pizza before it gets cold."

"I probably need to change Daph. Seems to go along with eating."

"Ain't that the truth," he remarked. "I'll do it. Just eat something, lady. I'll be right back."

She had to admit it was nice to have him take over and allow her to eat a relaxed meal. Sometimes when Daphne slept, she managed to uncoil a bit, but this was all still new enough that her brain had a habit of throwing up things to be concerned about. Would she ever stop listening for every little sound, or wondering when the baby was too quiet if she was still breathing?

Babies are hardy, the pediatrician had said today, echoing what Blaine had told her at their first meeting. After two weeks in her inexperienced hands,

Daph seemed to have proved that, even though Diane couldn't quite seem to believe it.

"She's sleeping," Blaine said as he returned to the kitchen. He'd learned his way around during the great changing table affair and pulled a plate from the cupboard. Two tall foam cups sat on the table, and he pushed one to her. "I hope you like diet soda, because that's what I brought. If not I can make some tea."

"It sounds good, actually." She smiled and took one of the cups, ripping the paper off a straw and poking it through the lid. Tingling cola soon hit her tongue. "Oh, yum. I don't have this very often. And the pizza is great. Thank you."

"Great, she says after one bite." He winked. "I've found pizza to be very much a matter of taste, having eaten it everywhere it seems to have spread. I even hear that people from New York and Chicago can disagree about it quite vehemently."

"I'm not so picky. And this is just fine, as far as I'm concerned."

He nodded and helped himself to a slice. "What was your experience of our planning board?"

She looked up and hesitated.

"Go on," he said. "I don't squeal."

"I'm not sure yet what they really want," she admitted. "Bigger and better, but bigger and better what? For example, they seem to be keen on historic preservation, but when we got to discussing the overlay, they got really fuzzy. I can't decide if they're not sure or don't want to offend some people."

"Probably both," he answered after he swallowed. "Big ideas are easy to come by. Implementing them, not so much. I guess that's your job."

"To an extent, yes, but I also serve many masters."

He laughed a bit at that. "I hear you."

"You've been awfully busy this week, too, haven't you?"

"Getting ready for winter. We have some other culverts that don't look as if they could withstand the weight of a plow, so they'll be replaced. Then there's a road that's in the plan to be paved, but the ranchers don't want it because it'll increase the traffic and they're worried about livestock."

She finished another bite of pizza before asking, "Are they right about the traffic?"

"They may be. This was in the original master plan to be widened and paved, and it would certainly make a grand link between two other roads that are heavily traveled. It's needed from that perspective. I've been considering it, however, and while I think it would be useful in a lot of ways, I'm sure it might cause problems in others. I'll show you next week when you can find time, and you can add your thoughts, if you don't mind."

"I probably should take a look at that and a lot of other things before I get into writing a new comprehensive plan. The other things being what the board members want."

"They want the moon and some green cheese, too."

That made her laugh. It also snapped her thoughts to him in a way that had nothing to do with Daphne or work. God, he was good-looking, she thought. He wore all that perfectly carved masculinity with a kind of comfort that said he wasn't even aware of it.

Brilliant blue eyes with black hair would always be arresting, but the rest of him begged the same attention. Broad shoulders, strong arms, large hands that appeared roughened from work. When he stood to hold Daphne, he displayed a flat belly, narrow hips and thighs that could have used a little more room in those jeans. And when he turned around... Man, she'd never have believed that she could admire a guy's rump.

While she'd noticed men occasionally since leaving college, she hadn't devoted a lot of attention to them, because all too many of the ones she met worked with her.

And now here she was again. Crap.

"You ever marry?" she asked Blaine, then wondered what had possessed her. It was none of her business, for one thing, and it tracked too closely with her edgy, almost squirmy awareness of his masculinity. Some areas of conversation ought to be avoided.

"No," he answered, then reached for a second slice. "Haven't managed to fit it in. Or maybe I just haven't felt drawn to the right woman. Can't say I've been lacking."

She quickly stuffed another mouthful of pizza in to silence the inevitable following question. *Don't ask.*

But a smile caught at the edges of a mouth she seriously would have liked to kiss—and wasn't that unusual for her?—and he answered as if he had read her mind.

"Lacking what, you'll be asking."

She pursed her lips as she swallowed. "I never said that."

He chuckled. "As night follows day. I told you about my experience with Ailis. I'm not the sort to be once burned and twice shy, as the saying goes, and I did dip my toes in the water. As it happens, I never met anyone else who made me want to take another deep dip of that kind. Which is not to say I've been a saint. I do believe Patrick was the last true saint on the isle."

A giggle spilled out of her. "Blaine, you're something else." A quiver ran through her as he smiled back at her. The way that expression reached his eyes just melted her.

"Well, to be honest about it, we grew a fair share of saints in the old days. The very old days. The rest of us weren't quite convinced, it seems." He winked. "Now me mam, she was always one for appealing to the Blessed Mother. I told you that. But it didn't keep her from wearing Saint Brigid's medal, I can tell you."

She liked the picture he was painting of his family. For all he said they'd spread out all over Europe, she got a strong sense from the way he talked that they were still very close. She'd missed that, as she'd missed a whole lot, it seemed.

"What about you?" he asked. "Family other than your cousin? Boyfriends? Exes?"

She looked down, losing her appetite. How in the world did you tell a man like this that you'd pretty much disowned your own parents? "My dad died when I was seventeen. Heart attack. I haven't seen my mother in years."

He didn't say anything immediately, for which she was grateful. It always sounded so bad when she said it, and it seldom helped when she explained that after her relationship with Max had turned so bad, she'd gone for counseling. It was the counselor who'd helped her to understand how her parents had poisoned her and set her up for Max's abusiveness. Or that her own mother and father had never stopped tearing her down.

"That must have been bad," he finally said. "I've seen families that were…toxic. Is that what happened?"

"You could say so. I don't know. I'll never know why I wasn't good enough for them."

She pushed her plate aside, and reached for her beverage. Her mouth had gone completely dry. "This isn't a therapy session," she said flatly. "Sorry."

"No need. It helps me understand why you're so constantly afraid of failing Daffodil, though."

Her heart skipped and she looked at him. "What do you mean?"

"Things you say. It's not like this is just something new you need to master..."

"Well, it is," she argued. "And I tend to master new things."

"Clearly, or you wouldn't have come so far in your career. No, it's the way you often seem to think you must be wrong or *will* be wrong with Daphne. Well, you've had her over two weeks and she's still with us, so you can't be failing."

Her discomfort was growing, but it was no longer from sexual awareness. This man seemed to be penetrating her mind, looking inside into places she tried not to disturb. How had she revealed so much? What was more, she still had plenty of reason to fear failing with Daph. There were a whole lot of years and a whole lot of opportunities to make serious mistakes ahead of her.

Having this child had made her aware of things she hadn't thought about it a long time, things she'd thought she had ditched after her counseling. Funny how some things only hid themselves away and never disappeared.

"You had a boyfriend?" he asked. "I get the feeling he wasn't all that."

"He wasn't. Oh, at first I thought he was." She couldn't sit still any longer, so she stood up and began to clear away the remains of her dinner. "Then came the point when I realized I was in danger of marrying my parents."

"Wow," he said almost under his breath.

"Well, when you're raised by someone who hates you and makes you feel like a constant problem, you think you're much better off with someone who only makes you feel like you don't matter. I was endlessly criticized until I realized it felt like I'd never grown up and left home. So I left him."

"Good for you."

"Maybe." She stood at the sink with a plate in her hand, suddenly tempted to just smash it. But she never did things like that. Never.

All of a sudden, powerful arms wrapped around her from behind, hugging her close to a hard chest.

"Sorry I pried," he said in that voice so deep she could feel its rumble against her back. "I had no idea."

"How could you?" she answered, her own voice thin. Now she wanted to cry. Just a little kindness and she nearly tipped into tears. All these years, all the effort she'd spent to turn herself into a successful career woman and bury all the old scars, and here she was bleeding over her own kitchen sink.

This man had stripped her bare, and he hadn't even intended to. Was she that fragile?

She gripped the edge of the sink, and words burst forth, powered by old pain. "Do you know what it's like to look into your mother's eyes and realize she hates you? That she hates everything about you, from the way you look to the way you act?"

"Good God," he murmured. "Obviously I have no idea. But why would the woman hate you?"

"I don't know." She bit her lip until it hurt, trying to hold back unwanted tears. A festering wound had just ripped open, and while she'd thought it had healed long ago, apparently it hadn't. "I just don't know. I tried to be good, but I was never good enough. She could barely stand to be nice to me in front of other people."

"And your da? Did he do nothing?"

"Not really. He was often a cipher, as if he just wanted to stay out of the way, then he died when I was seventeen. But there was no mistaking it, Blaine. I'm not making it up. I felt the weight of my mother's disapproval constantly, and I heard the unending criticisms. If there was anything right about me, I never heard it."

He squeezed her, holding her a little tighter. "And you eventually cut them off. She's never tried to reach you?"

"Not once." She unleashed a shaky sigh. "God, I sound so self-pitying. In truth, it was a relief to cut those ties. To never again feel obligated to call, only to hear the impatience in my mother's voice because I was keeping her from something else. I kept hoping. I didn't want to believe it, and then I had to."

"Therapy?"

"Yeah. After Max. I realized my folks hadn't been wrong—there was something about me that wasn't right. Why else would I fall in with a guy who treated me like dirt? Then she asked me if he treated me differently than I'd been treated at home. It was like this big, black fog dissipated. All of a sudden I could see so clearly."

Blaine continued to hold her from behind, awaiting any sign she wanted to be set free and keeping one ear cocked for sounds from Daphne. He hoped the girl didn't wake just yet, because much as he wouldn't mind holding her and making faces and sounds to draw a smile from her tiny face, he knew Diane needed this time.

Whatever pieces of herself she was assembling and reassembling after confiding in him, she deserved the time to do it.

And he needed some time to be just plain appalled and furious on her behalf. He was no spring chicken, and in the closely knit community back in Galway, he'd seen a share of terrible parents. They inflicted different kinds of ills on their children. Some had to be pried out of the pub at closing time. Some had carried physical discipline to the point of outright abuse. Sad fact was, not everyone was cut out to be a parent, and not everyone wanted a child even if they had one.

The question he'd never been able to answer was, if they didn't want kids, why did they keep them? If Diane's parents felt she was a major problem, why not give her up? As far as he knew, there was no law against saying you couldn't be a parent. Usually that was better than the mistreatment that could come from resentment and hate.

No wonder Diane had bouts of uncertainty and wondered if she was properly caring for Daphne. She had no experience even from her own childhood. And apparently she'd been raised to believe she couldn't do anything right.

Well, that was evidently a freaking lie. Her résumé was brilliant—she probably could have had her pick of jobs, but she had wanted to come here to have more control, to try out her own ideas. A worthy goal, one he believed she'd succeed at, unless she crippled herself with doubt.

He was half tempted to find out where her mother was hiding and go give her a piece of his mind. Not that it would do an ounce of good for Diane. But sometimes the man in him wished it could find satisfaction with a good, solid punch.

God, she felt so good in his arms. As if she had been fitted to him specially. But she stirred a little, and as much as he didn't want to, he started to drop his arms.

She astonished him, turning around to lean into him. "Thank you," she said.

She was thanking him? For what? A hug that he'd probably enjoyed more than she had?

"Sorry for venting like that," she added.

"I wasn't minding. Just wishing I might be able to do something useful."

She sighed and closed her eyes, saying, "Blaine, a hug was the most useful thing in the world. It's not like the past can be changed."

"If someone figures out a way to change the past, we'll all be in trouble."

He felt her move until her cheek rested on his shoulder. "Sure about that?" she asked.

"Well, if everyone created a past that they liked, we'd be in a world of trouble, don't you think? Nothing would mesh with anything else. Pure chaos."

"I hadn't thought of that." Then she stirred again, and something like a small sound of humor escaped her. "You're good for me. You make me laugh."

"That'll be a good thing, most times."

But the moment had passed, and he felt her move again. She needed him to step back and she didn't want to push him. At least that's how he read it. He dropped his arms and took a step away. Then it occurred to him that he might have read her wrong, and that she might therefore read his movement wrong.

Life didn't need to be terrible, did it?

Should he say something? He didn't know, and he wasn't a man accustomed to holding his tongue.

"I still haven't gotten another chair for the living room," she remarked, taking an unexpected direction. "I hate seeing you sit on the floor."

"I don't mind it a bit. But tell me about that grand old recliner chair you have. It didn't come with the house, did it?"

She shook her head, smiling faintly. "It was my

father's. Don't ask me why, but I'm truly attached to it. Given my feelings about my parents, that seems odd."

"Maybe not so odd. Maybe you have some good memories of it and just don't recall them consciously."

"It's possible. I grew up feeling like I was some kind of problem for him, but he never hated me the way my mother did. Maybe he couldn't stand up to her. I'll never know."

She wrapped her arms around herself as if chilled, and shook her head as if she wanted to brush something away. "The last time I went home was for my father's funeral. His chair was out at the curb. That's how fast my mother wanted to be rid of him. Anyway, I called someone to pick it up, and I've carried it around ever since. Don't ask me why I can't let go of it."

"Maybe," he said carefully, "you realize he was as much your mother's victim as you were."

Her head snapped up a bit. After a minute or so, she murmured, "You might be right."

Then she glanced at him from the corner of one golden eye, a humorless smile curving the edge of her mouth. "Two women, sisters. MaryJo's mom, who was an alcoholic until she died and had a daughter so mentally ill she may never escape the hospital. And then my mother. I don't know if she drank much, especially after I left, but she was certainly pickling herself in some very ugly emotions. I wish I knew why. What did their parents do to *them*?"

He leaned back against the counter and folded his arms. "Would it help to know?"

"Maybe we're just full of bad genetic material."

"Hey!" He didn't like that, and he wasn't going to stand here silently and allow her to lump herself into a heap with some disturbed people. She was clearly fine, clearly talented, clearly kind. What else but kindness could have caused her to take on the baby?

She looked at him again. "Is it cold in here?"

He switched his attention immediately and realized she was right. "Maybe. I'll go find the thermostat. If the heater isn't keeping up, I'll check it for you."

She shook her head a little. "You shouldn't have to do that. I have a landlord who's supposed to handle that stuff."

"Sure, and how fast do ya think he'll get here? You and the girl can't spend the night cold."

The thermostat wasn't difficult to find in the short hallway that led to the small house's two bedrooms. It wasn't the newest device, but it was good enough to tell him the temperature was below where it was set and he didn't hear a heater running.

"I'm going to the basement," he called. "You stay with the daffodil, make sure she's warm."

The basement stairs were both narrow and steep, and creaky besides. He had to tip his head to avoid banging it on a rafter. At least there was a lightbulb that worked, though it cast little illumination when he pulled the string. Oh, look, there was an electric torch on the edge of the stairs. He wouldn't have bet that it would work.

But much to his surprise, it did. The beam was yellow, indicating the need for some new batteries, but it would probably be fine for relighting a pilot light, assuming that was the problem.

Unfortunately, that was not the problem. Age and dust had clogged the combustion air intake. The gas valve was turned to the open position, but he quickly realized, after several attempts to light the pilot, that the safety feature was shutting everything down. No air, no pilot, no gas.

He sat back on his heels, gauging the situation. He couldn't fix this tonight. Even the landlord, whoever he was, couldn't fix this tonight. This was going to call for someone licensed to do the job. He didn't want to risk a slipup by getting out of his own lane into someone else's. Being an engineer didn't mean he knew how to do everything. A simple fix to this, yeah. A teardown and rebuild, nah.

That left Diane and Daphne. No way could he leave them here. His own place wasn't large and it was mostly designed to suit him, but he could fit all of them in there for a night or two.

He gave it one more try, using a piece of metal to tap on the air pipe, but it didn't open up, and frankly if it had at this point, he wouldn't trust it.

Some major repairs were needed.

He climbed the stairs again, making a note to tell Diane not to even try to descend them, at least when she was alone here. It would be easy to take a serious fall. He made a second note to get new batteries for the torch, because it likely didn't have much more life in it.

He found Diane waiting near the top of the stair.

"No dice," he said. "It needs some new parts. Your landlord is going to have to hire a heating specialist. Code and all that. You should call him now so he can get started on finding someone. In the meantime I'll gather up things for you and Daphne."

She had just started down the hall, probably to use the phone, but she stopped and looked back at him. "What have you been planning, Blaine Harrigan?"

He almost blinked. How was it she suddenly sounded like his mother? Well, not exactly, but she sounded Irish for sure. Then he saw a devil light in her eye and realized she was teasing.

"For that, woman, I'm going to take you to me own place so the two of you can keep warm until this heater gets fixed. Now go call that landlord of yours."

Chapter Eight

Daphne, holding true to form, had no problem settling down for the night in the playpen that Blaine had brought along for her. It occupied most of the floor in his tiny living room, but Diane noticed he had an advantage: a sofa and a recliner-rocker that she instantly loved. She smiled up at him from its well-padded embrace.

"Let me guess. This is your favorite chair."

Blaine laughed. "Depends on what I'm doing. If I need to stay awake, that is definitely *not* my favorite chair."

He rented a place in a newish-looking apartment complex outside town that didn't seem very full. The apartment itself was…an apartment. A small kitchen with a bar between it and the living room, trying to make a small area seem more spacious. Three doors opened off the living room, two bedrooms and a bath. Not an inch wasted for a hallway.

It was cozy, though, and over time Blaine had added some personal touches other than the furniture. A very happy-looking and bushy golden pothos hung in the corner near the wide window, the only window here. She watched as he pulled the curtains against the night. Navy blue. His furniture was dark green. An interesting color combination from a man, she thought. She liked it, though.

"I've only got the one bed," he remarked, "but you're welcome to it. Fresh sheets this morning. I can sleep on the sofa."

"And I can sleep right here in your rocker. In fact, you may have to pull me out of it if you want it back."

He laughed. "We'll argue about that another time. I'm thinking about a hot drink, and we barely made a dent on that pizza. I'm going to heat a slice or two in the microwave. Would you like one?"

"The drink sounds good, but I don't feel especially hungry. Thanks."

Since the kitchen was only two steps away, around an open bar with cabinets overhead, he didn't exactly go away. She watched him put a kettle on the stove and ignite the flame beneath it.

"I'm going to scald the pot first," he remarked.

"Why?"

"Because once the pot is warm, the tea I make won't get cold so fast."

"Duh."

He laughed. "Even with heat on in here, it's feeling a tad cold. You want me to turn it up?"

"I'm fine and Daph is wearing her blanket sleeper." She turned her attention to the playpen and wondered if she was overdoing the pink-and-white thing. Daph had some yellow and pale green onesies and shirts with tights, but right now she looked like a heap of pink and white inside her sleeper blanket and with her little knit cap on her soft, fuzzy head.

"I wonder when she starts growing hair," she murmured.

"Everyone's different, I think. Should I search it online?"

It was Diane's turn to laugh. "It's all such a mystery to me. I love the soft little blond fuzz on her head. Someone at the learning center said it was just baby fuzz and not even real hair."

"I don't know about that. None of my brothers or sisters lost whatever they had when they were born. All but one, Saphia, had a pretty thick head of it. She had peach fuzz for the longest time. Daphne, on the other hand, has some very fine blond hair. A bit more than fuzz, I think."

Diane nodded, once again fixated on her daughter. Amazing how that little bundle of smiles and tears had become so central to her existence in such a short time. "The scar from her surgery is healing very well."

"I noticed. I'm betting it won't even show in a few months."

The teakettle whistled, and Blaine poured some of the boiling water into a pretty teapot that looked as if it might be very old. "Is that teapot an antique?"

"Me gran's. Mam insisted on sending it back with me after my last visit."

"Any special reason?"

"When I was young, before I became a grand pain in the arse, I used to sit and play cards with Gran and we drank a whole lot of tea together. Fond memories of that pot. And fonder memories of taking me Gran to the cleaners, as they say."

"What?" The word emerged on a surprised laugh.

"Gran taught me to play blackjack. I beat her, probably because I was a youthful cheat and could count cards."

Diane couldn't help grinning. "You must have been a scamp."

"So Mam said. Anyway, it's not really cheating to count cards, although I hear they'd like you to believe so in Las Vegas. Numbers were always easy for me. They float around in my head the way words do for others, I suppose."

He emptied the water from the pot, scooped in some loose tea, then refilled it with water. "Not long now."

Wistfulness filled Diane. "So you had your grandmother around when you were a child?"

He looked up from placing the cover on the teapot and topping it with a knitted cozy. "Aye, I was lucky. I take it you weren't?"

She shook her head. "I was just thinking how nice it must have been to play cards with your grandmother."

"'Twas all that. She passed when I was eight."

"And now you have her teapot."

"That I do."

After a bit, some timer seemed to go off in his head. He lifted the cozy from the pot, pulled two pretty cups close and began to pour the tea through a strainer into them.

"Ooh, I've never seen anyone do that except on TV."

"I'm guessing public TV," he joked. "Well, ya can use your teeth to strain it, but I've never been fond of that."

She giggled. "I'm sure I wouldn't, either."

A short while later he'd placed a saucer and cup of milky tea on the small table beside her, then took a post on the end of the couch that was catty-corner to her with his own cup and a hot slice of pizza on a paper plate. In the middle of the open floor in her playpen, Daphne slept blissfully.

Calm, comfortable and oh so right. A dream, she reminded herself. One she had once longed for. One she thought she had found briefly with Max, but that had been her own delusion. Living an image that had never been there at all. Not for real.

But this was real. She owned no part of it—she

was just passing through, a guest in Blaine's life—
but for the moment, she could dream.

Then a crazy thought passed through her mind.
She could do more than dream. She could actually
reach for it. It might come to nothing, especially
since she and Blaine were coworkers...

"Blaine?"

He looked at her.

"Is there some kind of prohibition in this city or
county against government workers..." As it struck
her what she was about to ask, she fell silent and
wished she had a huge eraser for the words that had
slipped past her lips.

"Prohibition?" he repeated. "Depends on what
you mean. Against relationships?" He paused, then
spoke carefully. "Our fire chief is married to our
arson investigator."

"Oh."

"And our sheriff is married to the county librar-
ian. I don't think it's encouraged, but I'm not aware
of any rule against it." He took a very large bite of
his pizza, as if to make it impossible to talk.

Diane quickly picked up her tea, noting for the
first time that it was served in a dainty, flowered
teacup, and took a couple of sips. "This cup is beautiful," she said, trying to escape the awkwardness
she had generated.

"That crockery was me gran's, too," he said,
sounding as if he hadn't quite swallowed that last
huge bite. "Remarkable woman." Then his voice

cleared as he finished swallowing. "And she'd have swatted me for talking with my mouth full. Anyway, a grand woman by my estimation. She taught me a few things."

Grateful for the subject change, she managed a smile. "Like?"

"Like, if you want something, go fer it or you'll never be getting it."

Her breath stopped in her throat. He hadn't changed the subject at all, and he knew exactly where she'd been headed. Or at least thinking about heading. God, the man was a devil, reading her thoughts as if they were on a marquee above her head. Except that she was probably more transparent than she wanted to believe.

He rose from the couch. "I think I'll have a bit more of that pizza. How's your tea? Want me to warm it?"

Feeling safe again, she passed him her cup and saucer and focused on the baby sleeping in the playpen. Daphne was all that mattered. Her daughter. She didn't need any additional complications.

Except that Blaine Harrigan was turning into a complication she wanted very much to add to her life. "You said you were having trouble with the historic overlay?" Safe subject.

"Some. And I told you I want to take you out this week to see the road we're supposed to pave. It's in the plan, so the planner ought to take a look at it before we start. The best we can do now that it's getting cold is oil and gravel. You know anyone who likes oil and gravel road surface?"

"When it hardens…"

"Ah, but getting there." He placed another cup of tea beside her. "It's crap, is what it is. For three or four months, the road department gets a constant stream of calls about the gravel dinging paint and glass. The plows won't be able to touch it until it's really hardened in, and given the time of year, how likely is that? I ask you, who in their right mind decided that needed to be done *now*?"

She stared at him in some amazement, or maybe it was amusement. She'd never imagined him on a rant like that.

He put his fresh cup of tea on the table between them and the paper plate full of steaming pizza on his lap.

"Someone ordered it?" That rather surprised her. "Who?"

"One of your board members. Ask me why. I don't know, but there's something in it for him as sure as I'm sitting here. Thirty-five may be young, but I've been around a bit, and things like this don't get ordered out of the blue for no reason. But since it's in the plan…" He shrugged. "Not much of an argument I can make except it would be better to wait until next summer."

She hesitated. "But I could make a better argument?"

"I don't know." He leaned a bit toward her. "But

you can sure take a look at the plan overlays. I'd like to know if there's something...special about a piece of land out there. Something that isn't part of a ranch, or that's been sold recently. Or has been put on the market."

"The clerk's office would be a good place to start."

He nodded. "I've got the parcel number. It must be a fairly large piece because of subdivision."

He was right about that. Subdividing parcels to sizes below thirty-five or forty acres could get awfully expensive, so unless there was a big profit to be made, it didn't happen. She wondered what the hell was going on out there.

"But it's Friday night," he said suddenly. "Let's leave work for Monday. If your landlord gets the heat fixed tomorrow, I'll help you put that crib together for Daph."

She smiled. "It almost seems superfluous. She's sleeping well enough in the playpen."

"She's also small right now and easy to lift. In a few months, I venture you'll be glad to be lifting her out of a crib."

He had a point. Then, without consciously making the decision, she went to sit beside him on the sofa. "Mind?" she asked.

Did he mind? All she did was sit beside him, not even close enough to touch, and he felt as if skyrockets were going off inside his head. Ridiculous, since they'd been close before while dealing with Daphne, but this was different. She had elected to be close to him, without the baby as a reason.

"Of course I don't mind," he said roughly. His thoughts danced back to their earlier conversation about prohibitions against relationships. She had brought it up. Was she thinking about it?

He wasn't stupid. He knew that some women found him attractive. They always had. He also knew that it rarely lasted. Even good-looking Irish guys came with flaws. For that matter, so did most women.

"You know," he remarked, trying to keep the moment safe unless she wanted it to become something more, "I used to think that somewhere out there was a perfect woman I'd find one day."

"Not Ailis?"

"Her perfection lasted a couple of weeks. Hormone surges wear off, especially when they're not reciprocated."

He was pleased to hear her chuckle quietly. "They do," she agreed.

"But over time I figured something out. I'm not a total eejit."

She glanced at him with a faint smile. "Not even a bit of a one."

"Of course I am. Everyone has a bit of eejit in them."

She turned a little in her seat and looked at him more directly. "This thing you figured out?"

"Oh, yeah. Sounds so obvious when I say it, but most things do. My blinding insight was that nobody's perfect. Nobody at all. Pointless to be thinking that someone had to be perfect. Truth is, someone only has to be perfect for *me*. And me for her."

Her golden eyes searched his face. "Perfect how?"

"Like two puzzle pieces. They won't be the same shape, they'll stick out in different places and have divots in others, but they fit together. In other words, I needed to be looking for someone whose quirks fit mine. A complementary relationship."

"No success, I take it?"

"I haven't been looking hard, to tell ya the truth." He thought about it for all of two seconds, then reached for her hand. When she didn't pull it away, he dared to lift it to rest it on his chest. "Gettin' older, I guess. What seemed so important fifteen years ago isn't dominating my decision making anymore. You?"

She surprised him by leaning into his shoulder. "Me neither. I am so glad to be done with my teens and early twenties. Now there's time for other things in my life. It's not essential to have a date for Friday night anymore. That used to seem so important, long ago. In fact it feels like another time, another life."

He nodded slowly, trying to tamp down his more primitive urges. Here he was talking about not being as randy as he once had been, but feeling as randy as he ever had. Dangerous. Folly. He needed to keep this intellectual. Sure, and hadn't he been trying to do that since this woman had entered his life? "I remember. Then it became more important to have friends. Which is not to say I don't like sex."

Was he mistaken, or did her color heighten a bit? "Same here."

"It's what pulls us together, sometimes," he said, trying for a philosophical stance he was far from feeling. "It's also not enough by itself."

She opened her mouth to say something, but at that moment, Daphne started waking with a quiet but irritated cry. "It's that time," she murmured. "Almost eleven, right?"

He craned his neck a bit so he could see the numbers on the microwave clock. "You'd be right about that." Babies had wonderful timing. He'd known that for years. He almost laughed, but was afraid that he might be misunderstood after the conversation they'd been having. Intellectual, all right, but dancing around the edges of dangerous territory.

Although he might enjoy getting dangerous with this woman…as long as she was willing.

Diane was diapering like a pro now. Blaine disposed of the soiled diaper while the bottle of formula heated a bit in a pan of warm water. Daph had decided to be fussy. Diane paced with the child in the crook of her arm and bounced her gently, all the while talking softly to her.

It wasn't working.

"She must be famished," he remarked. Without waiting for permission, he popped the cover off the fresh bottle and shook a couple of drops on his wrist. "It's ready."

Diane accepted the bottle with thanks and soon Daphne was working on it with great intensity, a little frown between her brows. He tried to remember if he'd ever seen his sisters or brothers frown at this age, but he couldn't remember.

Diane, however, still hadn't completely recovered from last week's excitement. "I hope nothing's wrong," she murmured.

"She's probably just a bit out of sorts. They *do* have moods, Di."

Her head jerked up to look at him, and then a laugh escaped her. That apparently annoyed Daphne, because she pulled her mouth from the nipple and let out a cry. It wasn't a problem, however, because as soon as the bottle was offered again, she took it. Trying to hold it with her own two little hands.

"Before you know it," Blaine remarked, "she'll be feeding herself, running around in short tight skirts and even shorter shorts and wondering what she ever needed you for."

Diane flashed a grin. "I wasn't thinking that far down the road."

"No, but I saw enough of 'em grow up to have a notion how fast it happens. Kind of amazing, actually. You're living on your own clock, doing a hell of a lot of things with your life and every time you pause to look, you realize they're taller, smarter and more smart-mouthed…"

"Oh, stop," she said, humor making her voice tremble. "That's a long way away."

"Just keep tellin' yersel' that."

When Daphne was finished with her bottle, Blaine offered to take over. "I didn't realize how much I'd missed this," he remarked as he lifted her against his shoulder and took his turn at pacing with her.

"She certainly looks wide-awake now," Diane remarked. "It's a whole different view from back here."

"Usually is."

His old mates back home, and maybe even some of his buddies here, might have found it a bit odd for him to be going all soft over an infant and wanting to hug her like this. Ah, well. Sometimes he thought men could be absolute eejits about the things that mattered. Besides, he'd seen enough tough nuts crack when they had a kid of their own. Funny how that worked.

He decided to talk about something safe for now, something that would give him the opportunity to settle his urges. "If that heater gets fixed—or even if it doesn't, actually—want to take a scenic drive into the mountains tomorrow? I mentioned that old gold-mining town and the scenic road they want to build. Regardless of whether they do a damn thing about it, it's still a grand drive, and the daffodil will probably sleep through the whole thing, giving you a break."

"Sounds wonderful." She smiled. "I'd like to see it."

"Can't go walking around the ghost town. Too

many tunnels under it, and some are collapsing. If they want to make that a tourist destination, some work is going to be required to make it safe. But it would be a draw, I admit. It already is for the brave of heart. Anyway, don't look at it as part of the job. Just enjoy it. It's a beautiful drive this time of year."

At last Daphne settled and seemed ready to go back to sleep. She waved her arms and legs a few sleepy times, as if trying to hang on to wakefulness, but it didn't work. Almost as soon as she returned to the playpen, she drifted off into sleep.

Blaine and Diane wound up back on the couch watching her. After a bit, Blaine laughed quietly. "They tend to be the center of attention. Listen, I put fresh sheets on the bed when I got up this morning. It's yours. You have to be getting tired."

He saw it then, that hesitation, as if she didn't want to leave the daffodil that far away. Typical mom stuff. It probably killed her to leave the girl in day care. He guessed Diane was being subsumed by her new maternal role. Normal enough, but it wouldn't leave room for much else.

Aw, to hell with it, he thought. Nothing quite like the wrong time. "You must be knackered. If you don't want to use my bed, let me get you some blankets."

And what the devil had he been hoping would happen, anyway? The pull he felt toward this woman didn't mean she felt the same, even though he'd sometimes sensed it. Hell, she'd even asked about relationships between employees, so she was thinking about him at least a little.

He wasn't ordinarily shy about taking a stab at it, to see if there was any reason to continue, but this time he felt incredibly awkward. First off, he had to work with her, and a mistake of this kind could create problems all the way down the long corridor of time for both of them. Second, there was Daphne. He'd become remarkably fond of the tyke, and he didn't want to be obliged to stay away.

He opened the hall closet and began to pull out a blanket and pillow for Diane so she could be comfy on the couch. Then he changed his mind. Enough with all the dithering. She could speak for herself. Him holding one-sided arguments inside his head wasn't likely to settle anything.

He shoved the blanket and pillow back, then strode down the hall. Diane hovered over the playpen, at once beautiful and almost sylphlike. Looking at her now, it was hard to imagine the mountains of determination that had brought her to this point: a successful urban planner, a mother to her cousin's child. She might look fragile at this moment, but this woman was made of steel.

When she realized he was just standing there, she looked up from the baby. "Blaine?"

"Will ya come ta bed wi' me?" His accent had burst out of its confines, and he didn't care.

She could have had any reaction at that point and he wasn't sure any of them would have surprised him, from throwing him out of his own place to announcing she was moving to the motel.

But she chose none of those answers. Instead she glanced down once more at Daphne, then rounded the playpen until she stood right in front of him. "I think that's the most romantic proposal I've ever had."

"I doubt it. It wasn't romantic at all. It was the words that popped out of me addled brains. And you're the one addling them."

Her smile seemed to hold a cat's contentment. "I like the sound of that."

He was still dealing with his surprise that she hadn't told him where to stuff it, his coming on to her like that. "I need to work on it."

Her smile deepened. "Just one promise, Blaine."

"And that?"

"If we mess up everything tonight, we act like it never happened. I don't want to lose your friendship."

And with that she set off all the fireworks in his head until he felt like Marco Polo making the biggest discovery of all: gunpowder. "I can promise that."

Hell, he'd managed to carry on as if Ailis hadn't told him where to leave his head, and in front of his best lads, too. Yeah, he could promise that, but damned if he was going to allow it to happen. No muck-ups tonight.

He'd had enough experience with women to feel safe in promising that.

"The main thing," he muttered, "is to listen."

"What?" The word sounded as if it had been surprised out of her, but he was past talking. Hell, he'd been past talking for hours now. He'd done his best to keep that ball rolling, to prevent anything risky from happening…but here he was, walking right into it and feeling the heat growing between them like an explosion about to go off.

Only one dim bulb was on in the room, just enough to prevent a catastrophe in the middle of the night.

But despite the lack of light, his gaze drank her in, every detail, from the gentle mounds of her breasts that were just hinted at beneath her flannel shirt to the delicate curve of her neck.

The day he'd first seen her, frazzled as she'd seemed, he'd tried hard not to notice the way the silky folds of her blouse draped over her, suggesting without shouting.

Every move she had made in that outfit, from her blouse to her slacks to the stray blond hair that had teased her cheek, had reached out to him like an invitation.

He'd buried his reaction almost before he knew he was having it. He had perhaps let thoughts of this day trail across his mind from time to time, but had firmly squashed them. He didn't need an announcement to understand that she must be nearly overwhelmed between a new job and a new baby. She didn't need additional complications.

Yet here she was, her golden eyes dimmed in the

poor light, clearly longing for him yet getting more nervous as he stood here like a dolt letting the moment wash over him in its myriad sights, sounds and feelings.

"I've wanted you," he said as quietly as he could, the sounds emerging from the depths of his chest, "from the moment I saw you."

Her smile returned, looking less nervous. "While I was frazzled with a baby? You had to take over the diapering. What man finds that sexy?"

"A man who isn't put off by babies but has just been confronted by one of the most beautiful women he's ever seen."

"Beautiful?" She almost gasped the word. "None of your blarney, Blaine Harrigan."

"I never kissed the stone." But her teasing mood relieved his unusual paralysis. Could it be that he was worried about whether he would love her well enough? Only one way to find out.

He'd have liked to pick her right up off her feet and carry her to his bed, but this bloody doorway wasn't wide enough. For an instant he thought of that ranch he'd considered buying, and most of all a sprawling homestead with more room than any house he'd ever been in. But that all slipped away as he took her small hand in his bigger one and gently urged her toward the bedroom.

Her shyness and nerves seemed to have dissipated. Once inside his room, she came into his embrace as naturally as if she'd always been there. His own muscular size, built through years of manual labor that around here was as much a part of his job as the desk work, made him acutely aware of how fragile this woman was. Not weak, but fragile. A being requiring gentleness from him in every way. Gentleness he wanted to provide.

Bending his head, he sought her mouth for a kiss. Hard to believe they had come to this without any sexual exploration. Blame Daphne for that, he thought with mild amusement.

But amusement quickly vanished, along with most rational thought, as she opened her mouth to him, inviting him into the warm, moist depths of her very being. Excitement slashed through him, sharp desires that reached his every cell. His tongue was his surrogate, but thrusting in and out of her, tracing the pearls of her teeth, tasting the faint remnants of tea, didn't feel less than total penetration. It felt like the first small step to completion.

Joy joined passion, elevating him until thought very nearly vanished, giving way to feeling. Her arms slid around him, then clamped tightly, her nails digging into this back as if she were hanging on for dear life. Never had he felt so *needed*.

One of her hands slid upward, capturing the back of his neck, turning him into her prisoner. The other slid down and around until she was working at his belt buckle.

She didn't want any fooling around. She was in a mad rush, too.

With effort, he lifted his head. Her eyes fluttered open, looking sleepy. "Blaine?"

"Do we need to be hurrying?" Fast, slow, he didn't care for himself.

"Hell, yes," she said, then clamped her mouth to his once again.

Well, then…

She pulled away and surprised him by beginning to shed her own clothing. He could take a hint, and he stripped his quickly.

Then there was the breathtaking moment, absolutely breathtaking, when all the barriers were gone. The chilly air made her nipples pucker, large nipples with the pinkest of areolae. Her waist tapered down to a woman's hips, not a boy's, with all the curves he so admired, curves that would cradle him, not fight him.

Gorgeous. Farther down he found her long, lithe legs, yet like so much of her, curved, too. No protruding knees, no sign of the underlying bones, absolutely perfect.

The air in the room seemed to be thinning out as he filled his eyes with her naked beauty. Had he created her out of the stuff of dreams, she could not have pleased him more. In response, the electric ribbons of desire that ran through him became more like a primitive drumbeat. His staff was erect, and it twitched in time to his need.

He hoped he pleased her half as much as she pleased him.

He needn't have wondered. "You're perfect, Blaine."

No, not perfect, he thought. The scars of brawls, of minor accidents, of careless moves with a tool... they marked him all over.

She stepped closer and touched a crescent scar on his upper thigh. "What's this?"

The moment almost slipped away, interrupting passion with one of his least favorite memories from childhood, but she deserved an answer. That was one too big to ignore. "Me and some of the lads were riding our bicycles down a hill out a way in the country. We liked it because we could go fast. Too fast."

"Oh, no!" She looked at him, concern on her face.

"As you can see, I'm fine."

"But it was close, wasn't it?" Then she deprived him of reason and thought by cupping him in her hand. He sucked air between his teeth. "Am I hurting you?"

"You're a witch," he growled, and before she could do more, he grabbed her, twisted her and threw her on the bed on her back. "So we want games, do we?"

A small laugh escaped her. "What kind of games do we have in mind, Mr. Harrigan?"

He was sure liking this playful side of her. He straddled her, leaving everything exposed to the gods and her. Then he grabbed her wrists and forced them to the top of her head, where he held them easily with one hand.

"I could make you my prisoner," he rumbled. "An offering on the altar of my desires." He began to caress her from neck to privates, noting how silky she felt everywhere. At once she began to squirm in response, and little gasping breaths started to escape her. "Too much to handle?" he asked, teasing.

"Try me," she gasped back. "Just try me."

"Oh, I intend to." Caressing her with his hand while she wriggled delighted him. Amazingly responsive, and he was enjoying the way she felt beneath his touch.

Electricity seemed to fill the air, feeding his wants and desires as if he were plugged into a power source. Anticipation gripped him with yearning, and an unexpected fear that she might change her mind.

But with a strong pull, she broke his hold on her wrists and her hands landed on his chest, as light as butterflies, but maddening as she slowly began to trace him. A lazy smile curved her mouth as she closed her eyes and gave herself up to the world of sensation.

"I want you," she whispered. "I'm aching with it. Every part of me is alive to you…"

He could say the same, and began to feel a subtle shudder growing in his arms and legs as strength gave way to a stronger need.

Her hands cupped him again, dragging a deep groan from him, then she stroked his erection, nearly driving him to the edge of insanity.

"Witch," he muttered. Ah, by the saints, he couldn't forget…

Rolling onto one elbow, which brought his hips

into electric contact with her, he pawed in the night-stand drawer, hoping the condom wasn't too old…

She grabbed it from him, struggling to rip it open, then with a pleased smile began to roll it onto him. Nobody, ever, had done that for him, and he never would have dreamed that it could be about the sexiest thing a woman could do.

"Damn," he said without apology, then lowered himself, seeking her welcoming cavern, until he felt the instant where they met and she gave him entrance.

Slowly, savoring his plunge toward ecstasy, ignoring the way her hands gripped his hips and pulled on him, he savored every single split second of their union.

Then at last he was deep within her. Filling her. Claiming her. Uniting them in bliss.

Diane hadn't had long to be surprised by her own boldness. She'd never felt this way before, but something about Blaine drew it out of her, a woman filled with power and her own desires who refused to be denied. If he had turned away…

But he hadn't. He had answered her desire with his own, which was clearly every bit as strong.

There was something very special about Blaine wanting her, but she couldn't sort through that now. Soon she was awash in passion, anticipation and an edgy sort of fear that none of this would really happen, that something was going to tear these moments out of her grasp.

It seemed so impossible…

But as his touches ignited bonfires all throughout her body, she stopped fearing and started experiencing, filled with joy and wonder and a hunger unlike any she had ever known.

Then…then he was deep within her, filling a place too empty for too long, stretching her in ways that made fresh thrills run through her, and a satisfaction that was almost enough by itself.

But not enough, as he soon proved, moving within her, lifting her from reality in a world populated by sensations beyond description, sensations that blinded her, drove her, hung her on a precipice she feared she might not be able to fall over.

But finally, finally, with one deep thrust, he tossed her over that edge into free fall among the stars. She heard his groan as he shuddered, but it merely added to the almost painful sensation of falling into heaven.

Chapter Nine

Blaine fell asleep with Diane wrapped in his arms. He'd murmured sweet things to her, caressing her hair and side gently, telling her how wonderful she was, but then the inevitable happened.

Amused, feeling absolutely wonderful and not at all abandoned, she woke from her own doze and rose and quickly pulled on her undies, socks and flannel shirt. The digital clock beside the bed said it was nearly five, and Daph had yet to miss her five o'clock feeding.

The apartment was a little chilly, but not too much so. She began warming Daphne's bottle in a pan beside the sink and listened to the wind whip up outside. A change in weather coming?

Having recently come from Des Moines, she figured she had enough cold weather gear for herself, but the baby? She'd need to go shopping again.

A trickle of amusement filled her. Nobody had warned her how expensive a baby could be. Especially starting from scratch. Bed, playpen, changing table, mobile, toys, blankets, new clothes as she grew and now winter wear. Oh, and don't forget the mountain of disposable diapers and the formula.

She now seriously understood the point of a baby shower.

There was still some tea in the teapot, probably really strong by now, but she used the strainer and poured some into a coffee mug, not willing to risk Blaine's grandmother's china in a microwave.

Just as she pushed the buttons to heat it, she felt powerful arms slip around behind her.

"The bed was empty and getting cold," Blaine murmured in her ear.

A shiver of pleasure trickled through her. "It's almost five. Daphne's witching hour."

"I figured." He kissed her earlobe, then the nape of her neck, and released her, causing more delightful shivers. She hated to feel his arms slip away. "If it's tea you're wanting, I'll make fresh. That's past the point of drinking. It'd peel paint off a car."

She turned to face him, feeling the smile that danced around her mouth. "Fresh tea, then?"

"Coming up."

The tea was ready and steaming in delicate cups

before Daph stirred. Diane started to move toward the playpen, but Blaine forestalled her.

"Let me? I've been missing the babes. Missing family, come to that. Careful or I'll adopt ya both."

She didn't think that sounded so awful, but it was a luxury to be able to settle on the couch and sip her tea while Blaine tended to her daughter. She curled her legs under her, a favorite position she hadn't indulged often since Daphne's arrival, and pulled the afghan over the back of the couch onto her bare legs. Warm and cozy.

She loved looking at Blaine. So strong and good-looking, with that startling Irish combination of nearly black hair and brilliant blue eyes. But as much as she loved that, she loved seeing the way he cradled her daughter, murmuring to her, his attention completely fixed on her as he called her daffodil. Occasionally he even hummed.

And Daphne's gaze was as fixed on him, never wavering.

As Daph was nearing the bottom of her bottle, Blaine looked up. "I was thinkin'."

"Yes?"

"I was thinkin' I'd like to date you. Normal-type dating. Not just me running over to see what you might need, but taking you out to dinner or a film. I'd suggest dancing, but the roadhouses can get rough. Or you could come with me to my darts game and meet the lads."

She didn't know what to say. He wanted to *date*

her? That meant a lot more than the friendship that had been growing between them, never mind the time they had just spent in bed. That could be dismissed. Maybe. Butterflies began fluttering in her stomach.

"And in case you're worryin'," he continued, "Daph can come with us if you want. We'll just choose things that will be okay for her. Drives in the mountains before snowfall. There's even a ranch I've been mulling buying, and I wouldn't mind your opinion."

She was still trying to absorb all of this. Did this mean something more than friendship? Stupid question. He'd been then one to call them dates. She seized on the thing that seemed totally out of place. "Why would you want my opinion on a ranch? And why in the world are you even thinking about buying one?"

"Because it'd be a big spread of land, unlike anything I could get back home. When I was young and running on the streets and hills of Galway, I loved Western films. I kinda outgrew that, but I never lost my desire for owning a big piece of land and having horses. This place offers so many opportunities. It's a big country."

She nodded, thinking about it. "Years ago, back when I was in college, I went with some girlfriends on a camping trip. We wound up in the seriously misnamed Sunshine Campground."

"Why misnamed?" Daphne must had enough,

because he put the bottle aside and lifted her to his shoulder.

"Because the entire five days we were there, it never stopped raining."

He laughed. "Misnamed indeed."

"While we were there, anyway. The point is, we met a couple from Sweden. They'd planned to drive the country from one end to the other with plenty of time to stop and take in the sights, but they were only halfway across and running out of time. I remember how they kept repeating their astonishment that this country is so big."

"It certainly is, and I like it. If I got a ranch, I could bring me nieces and nephews for visits. They'd be agog at the space, and even more agog at being able to ride horses."

"I bet they would. I haven't ridden in years."

"Did you like it?"

"Loved it." She smiled feeling oddly wistful. "It was actually a course in college. My family never would have paid for regular riding lessons."

"Would you like to do it again? I happen to have a horse I stable with Gideon Ironheart. I'm sure you could ride her, or Gideon would gladly let you choose another mount."

She looked at him. "What in the world are you driving at, Blaine Harrigan?"

His smile spread. "I told you, I want to date you. I think we might have something going here, and there's only one way to find out. As for you looking at the ranch, I couldn't tell you the number of times I heard me mam complain about how men just couldn't see the most obvious things. I don't think she was talking about timber and framing."

Diane laughed. "Probably not."

"Anyway, no rush."

Dating. It sounded so formal. She remembered the first time she went out with Max. He'd had a couple of tickets to some show and said one was a spare. He'd asked her to come but carefully pointed out, *This is not a date.*

She should have walked away right then, but she'd taken it to mean they were just going as friends. Little had she guessed that he'd meant friends with benefits, which had evolved to something more and left her feeling emotionally slashed.

But she and Blaine had arrived at an entirely different place. They'd already had sex. Now he wanted to *date*? He must be trying to say something, but she wasn't sure what.

"What's wrong?" he asked.

She looked up from her lap and realized he'd stopped walking with Daph and was simply watching her while the baby slept against his shoulder.

"I don't know. I mean…dating seems like an afterthought now. Maybe?"

"Wasn't intended to." He sighed a bit, then walked to the back of the apartment. From the sounds she could tell he was changing Daph. When he returned, he placed her daughter in the playpen, and she was still feeling confused about what he was trying to get to here.

He sat beside her on the sofa and took her hand. "I never thought I was good at this sort of thing. Yeah, I dated a few women, and it never worked out and I always figured it was me. Ailis gave me a good idea of that. So you ask a woman out to dinner or to a film, she says yes and never calls you again and never returns your calls. Or…she just turns you down before you get the invite out of your mouth. Common enough, I s'pose."

"Likely," she agreed. "There's certainly nothing wrong with you that I can see."

"Sure and I'm God's gift, can't ya tell?"

That drew a small laugh from her. "Maybe not quite."

"Definitely not quite. Any road… Matters between us have been flowing backward."

That startled her. She twisted so she could see him better. "In what way?"

"Well…I walk into your life by way of the daffodil, and I'm busy falling for the child, and fixing up your nursery, handy lad that I am, so baby came first. Then…we worked together a bit here and there, but hardly so's you'd notice, and we still don't really get to know each other, and then the next step—we have sex. Not that I'm complaining, but aren't things supposed to happen in the reverse order? Me datin' you, us deciding a trip to bed would be grand, then me falling for your daughter?"

He had a point, but the way he framed it made a bubble of amusement rise inside her. She should have been nervous that he was looking for a way out of the rapidly growing intimacy between them, but he was instead looking for a more customary version of events.

"So we did it backward?"

He smiled, tilting his head a little. "I'm quite sure if you read one of them self-help books, you'd find we got it all wrong. Now me, I'm in the way of thinking that I'm very fond of you—and your daughter—but shouldn't we have some of the fun of getting to know one another over a bowling ball or a pint or a game of darts? Or if none of those interest you, over dinner or a drive in the country?"

She liked the idea. Part of her had somehow developed a deep craving for this man, and it wasn't just that she found him so sexually attractive. When she heard his voice in the hallway outside her office, she always looked up hopefully. Sometimes he poked his head in to say hello and she felt he'd made her day…which surely was over-the-top.

No question but she liked him. His question, however, seemed to be was there something more in this for both of them, and he was suggesting a way to find out. Slowly. Carefully. Taking their time. Having fun together.

Her gaze trailed to Daph, sound asleep in her playpen, and she had to agree that in a way Blaine was right. They'd come together quickly and strongly over her child, but there was so much more that was needed if they were to be more than a flash in the pan. It seemed he wanted a whole lot more than that.

He spoke again, tightening his hold on her hand just a bit. "I'm in the way of believing in love at first sight."

She drew a sharp breath and fixed her gaze to his face.

"But believing it, which I do, and trusting in it are two different things. I'd like to think that given time we'd build a future, not just the present."

"Wow," she whispered. In his words she heard a hope that almost felt like it could swamp her. On the other hand, she wanted it. She hoped this could grow, because the taste of it she'd had so far had made her remarkably happy.

"Anyway," he said, "just think about it. If it doesn't appeal to you, that's fine. Your choice."

Her choice? All of sudden she was frightened. So much had changed in her life so quickly—how could she possibly make a decision of any kind? She'd barely gotten used to being a mother, and she was still feeling her way into her job. She'd only fallen into all this with Blaine because he'd been helpful.

So much as it troubled her, she said quietly, "I need time, Blaine. I'm not ready to date. Too much has been changing too rapidly."

His smile shadowed a bit but didn't disappear. "I understand." He leaned back against the couch, still holding her hand. "I'd have fixed that heater for you later this morning," he said, changing the subject. "But it'd be better to have someone with a license do it. I think I said that. I'd hate to make some kind of mistake."

The silence in the room seemed to grow, consuming what had been a beautiful night.

It was all her fault. Tiny fingers of panic squirmed into her heart. Had she just made the biggest mistake of her life?

Then, making her feel even worse, he carried on as if nothing at all had happened. He made breakfast for them as the sun started rising and suggested they take that drive while the light was best.

"With any luck," he added, "we'll get back and find out you have heat and can move home again."

Yup, she thought miserably, she'd blown it.

Chapter Ten

A month later, Daphne was sitting up on her own and creeping around the playpen and floor like a pro. The baby laughed a lot and seemed quite happy with life.

Diane felt less so. She had friends now, women she could gather with on a Saturday afternoon, babies everywhere. She especially liked Ashley McLaren, Marisa Tremaine and Julie Archer, but the gals she'd met her first day, from the clerk's office, were also a lot of fun.

Little by little she was getting the information she needed from the members of the planning board, and by way of them from the city and county officials.

Talk about grandiose ideas. She wasn't sure most of the residents around here would be thrilled with the kind of growth these people envisioned, but that was the point of inviting those who would have an interest to a public meeting. Lots of ideas were bound to get shot down.

She was busy, Daphne was healthy and she should be thrilled with the way things were going.

Except for Blaine. He was still friendly, still popped in to talk to her at least once a day, and every weekend he stopped in to lavish love on his "little daffodil." During those times, they talked quite a bit.

But she could feel a barrier between them, something that had slipped into place quietly when she had said she didn't want to date.

That lay entirely at her door, and in one sense she didn't regret her decision. Her life had been jampacked with changes, and she didn't want to make him a crutch, which she could have easily done, as helpful as he'd been. No, she'd been in no position then to even consider something as important as whether they should date.

While it was true that dating was a far cry from marriage, it carried certain obligations with it. And if it didn't work out, someone was bound to get hurt. So she guessed she'd been the one who'd raised the barrier, but he was definitely observing it.

What she hadn't expected was that with passing time, it didn't get easier. Far from it. She was beginning to hurt. But in no way did she get the sense from him that he felt the same. Except for his attention to Daphne, he appeared to have moved on and to be satisfied with friendship.

Well, why not? As he'd pointed out, they really hadn't had time to get to know one another. Not then. He'd proposed dating as a way to do that, and she'd shut him down. Worse, she'd probably made him feel the way Ailis or Alice had years ago. He'd reached out and been slapped away because of her stupid concern that she was in no position to make a decision yet.

But she hadn't needed to decide anything. All she had needed to do was date him, see how things went. He'd been frank about that.

He'd also been right that they'd started everything backward. Even now his description of putting the cart before the horse could amuse her.

Time had passed, however, and the feeling that she'd made an awful mistake kept growing. She began to lie awake at night, wondering if it was too late to change her mind.

It hardly seemed possible that autumn was nearly over. The leaves had lost their color, and most had fallen from the trees. In town, diligent people raked them into leaf bags or blew them away to somewhere.

She enjoyed some amusement when she was out walking Daph in her new stroller, to think of the chain link of leaf blowers sending the crackling debris on a steady trip out of town.

Daphne apparently hadn't reached an age yet where she was ready to be terrified by anything new, because she seemed to enjoy even the noisy leaf blowers or the occasional roar of a passing vehicle that needed a muffler job. Everything tickled her. She waved her hands and made happy sounds that came pretty close to giggles.

Diane wondered if she'd been this happy as a baby. Once she started growing up, she sure hadn't been. But she was determined that Daphne would be loved and appreciated in all the ways she herself hadn't been. One way to learn parenting was to learn all the things not to do, she thought wryly.

It was Sunday afternoon, and Blaine had called last night to ask if he could come over. That was making her uncomfortable, too, that he felt he needed permission to pop in. None of her other new friends seemed to feel that way.

He was sitting on a plastic chair on the porch, one of those molded things that were cheap and she'd figured would do for now. He stood up when he saw them coming and waved, smiling.

Damn, he looked good enough to eat. Feeling the pull toward him as strong as ever, maybe stronger, was like a wake-up call to her stubborn brain. She hadn't stopped wanting him, and her reasons had all been a sham. She was afraid she would fail, ruin any kind of relationship with Blaine. She didn't think she could stand that failure.

He came down the two steps and picked up the stroller, lifting it easily onto the porch, all the while talking to Daph in something approaching baby talk, which she had to admit sounded a wee bit strange emerging from a man whose voice rose from the bottom of his chest.

"I brought you a surprise, Daffodil," he was saying as he unbuckled her from her stroller. "I used to have one when I was little like you, but they're hard to find these days."

Diane couldn't help but smile as she watched the big man lift her daughter and watched Daphne smile and chortle in response to his voice. There was a bond there now, no two ways about it.

Inside, she offered him tea as he shed his jacket and began to remove Daphne's warm sack and knit cap from her. "She'll need mittens almost before you know it. Yes, I'd fancy that tea, if you don't mind. Everything still sailing smoothly for you?"

"Have you heard anything to the contrary?"

Blaine didn't immediately answer then said, "Is that sarcasm or a real question?"

"Probably both," she admitted as she grinned at him. In the kitchen she put the kettle on, and he sat at the table with Daphne on his thigh. "I've been digging into things. I'm not exactly sure of all I've found. Some of it feels a bit…archaeological."

That drew a crack of laughter from him. "That I can believe. No, I haven't heard a word against you, at all. You seemed to have buttered them up well."

"I hope so. We aren't going to get a damn thing done if they're mad at me. And you haven't really mentioned culverts, for all the times you've dropped by."

"We're fixing the ones that most need it. Take it from me, it's going to be a mess come spring. A lot of places don't have much life in them." He paused, then added, "I hope that one of these days soon you'll be able to do that historic district lookover with me. We really need to get that sorted."

She flushed faintly because she realized she'd been avoiding that—he'd asked her when she first got here. Yes, there were things she needed to settled with the city government, but she also needed some idea of what she needed to push for. "Soon," she heard herself promise.

"Good. Now the pressy for Miss Daffodil here." He reached into a deep pocket on his work shirt. In fact, the shirt had all kinds of pockets, looking more suited to a photographer of old, but most of the pockets appeared to contain something.

Out of one he pulled a small sheaf of cloths. Suddenly curious, Diane leaned closer. "Is that a cloth book? I don't think I've seen one in forever."

"It is, and I had to be ordering it online. Seemed strange to me. They were common enough when I was helping raise up the youngsters. Anyway, while you make us that tea, I'm going to read her first book to her."

Diane listened, charmed, as he read the very simple story to her, which included lifting flaps to reveal new objects. Daphne probably didn't understand a bit of it, but she enjoyed the colors, the changing scenery and…might as well face it, Blaine's attentions.

"I wouldn't leave her alone with it till she's older," he said when he finished and folded the book up, holding it so Daphne could explore it with her hands. "It's supposed to be safe, but I wouldn't be trusting that just yet."

"I agree," she answered and didn't resent the suggestion in the least. He seemed as much a part of Daph's life now as she did, and Diane felt not the least bit of possessiveness. Well, Blaine had been here almost from the very start.

She glanced toward the window and saw the early evening was beginning to shade the world. "I was going to make a small roast for dinner. Join us?" It was the first time she had asked him to stay for dinner since she'd dropped the hammer on him. Not even the next day when he'd assembled Daph's crib for her.

"I'd like that," he said, granting her a smile before returning his attention to the baby.

She stared glumly for a few moments, then started making the tea. He only came around for Daphne. He'd lost all interest in her, and she couldn't blame him for that.

When she'd set the mugs on the table, along with a saucer for the tea bags, she sat across from him and watched him tease Daphne by waggling his index finger around until she reached up and caught it. Then she didn't want to let go.

Oh, she had a way with him, she thought. A way with her, too. And now she wondered if she could even force the words past her dry mouth. But... she wanted him with an ache that was still growing rather than diminishing, and it was hard to accept the responsibility for having broken any chance they might have had. Fear, she thought. Fear of failing once again. Was that to hobble her entire life? It had certainly made a mess of this.

She rose and pulled the roast out of the refrigerator. A beef roast was an extravagance she seldom indulged, but every so often the serious carnivore in her emerged. She'd even bought an extra baking potato, too, so she had enough.

But it wasn't time to start cooking yet, she realized. She was just going to have to live with any awkwardness.

"That land you were wondering about?" she said as she sat at the table again.

"Which?"

"Alongside the road that the board suddenly wants paved with oil and gravel."

"A bad thing to be doing before late spring, and so I told them. They didn't like it, but they didn't want the problems I described, either. Did you learn something?"

"Yes. I went after it because of the new comprehensive plan. It's been subdivided. One of the county commissioners is part of an investment group that wants to build a strip mall there."

"There?" Disbelief edged his voice. She couldn't blame him. "Have they lost their bloody minds? The middle of nowhere?"

She had to smile, and in smiling let go of the tension that had tightened every nerve ending in her body. There were worse things than only being friends with this man, such as not being friends with him at all. "You said it joined two major roads, correct?"

"Ya. But it exists only so ranchers can move stock and supplies around. The master plan was totally vague on any other use."

"Well, it's not vague anymore." She sighed and leaned her elbows on the table. Boy, did Daph look happy on Blaine's lap, surrounded by one of his powerful arms. She made little noises and the waving of her arms had become more purposeful. She wanted that book.

"Meaning?" he asked.

"Apparently there aren't a whole lot of services on the northern road, and the southern road, well, you have to take some twists and turns to get to town. Somebody must think that a gas station, convenience store and small restaurant could make some money there as long as they have signs on the main roads giving directions. But of course they can't get the financing until they have a road in good enough condition to handle construction traffic. After it's all built, there's some hinting around that it could be paved into a two-lane."

He drummed the fingers of his free hand on the tabletop. The sound made Daphne giggle. "I'm quite certain that isn't in the current master plan."

"Nope," she answered. "But the pressure to get it into the one I'm working on is how I learned about it."

He frowned. "Did you just write it in?"

"Of course not, Blaine! I'm not the ruler of this county, and despite the pressure I started to feel, I pointed out that we needed to have a charette with all the affected property owners."

"Charette?"

"Public meeting. Everyone who'd be affected— we call them stakeholders—gets the opportunity to see the proposal and comment on it. That slowed down the push, I can tell you. But I didn't get the whole story until this past week. I've been edging around it, but I wasn't getting anywhere until I finally said I could see no point in turning that road into some kind of artery. Not enough traffic. Didn't your friends at the road department tell you we'd been taking a traffic count?"

He nodded. "But I didn't think much about it when I heard. I'd had my victory. No paving before spring. A strip mall? Where the devil did they find investors willing to go for that out there?"

"That I don't know. Their construction plans are my business only to a point. You know that. Providing a comprehensive plan gives me some input, but we won't be looking for grant money for something like this, so…" She shrugged. "I need to get everyone who'll be affected by this together before we write it into the plan. I think I ticked off at least one board member, but there's a lot in the scale now. They hired me because their plan was so outdated they couldn't get grants. Heck, it was in violation of more regulations than I can count. So they can't just sweep this under the rug. They might be able to push through their strip mall before the new plan is ready for a vote, but it won't help in the long run, because I suspect there'll be a lot of environmental concerns that will have to be addressed regardless."

He nodded slowly. "You mean that the environmental requirements can't be ignored simply because they're not in the old plan."

"Exactly. It's not like the regulations come into being only when they're written into the plan." She sighed. "I've spent the better part of a week trying to get that across."

"And you survived?" He looked faintly amused.

"You bet. I told them they'd better get an impact statement before anything is touched, signed or paid for."

"This whole thing still feels weird." Daphne had drooled on his forearm, and he took a napkin from the basket on the table to dab it away, then dab at her mouth. She gurgled and reached again for the book. "Maybe I should put this away for another time."

But he didn't move, and neither did she.

"I'm sorry," Diane said after a few moments. "Here it is the weekend and I'm talking about work."

"I don't mind, actually. I've been so busy running around putting out fires that I haven't been able to keep up. I'm glad you filled me in. But I still don't get this whole strip mall idea."

"Me neither. Would you have any idea why Sagebrush Ranch would want to sell off that parcel?"

"Money. Ranching is a tough business these days."

Daphne's head was nodding. Blaine rose. "Bed or playpen?"

"Either one. I doubt she'll sleep long. She's staying awake more in the daytime."

A significant change, Diane thought as she rose and went to look over her dinner choices. A three-pound beef roast was about as small as she could cook in the oven and hope to have it done just right. She hated when it grew so overcooked it tasted like cardboard. Plus, she loved cold roast beef sandwiches for lunch.

Then a wave of longing hit her so hard she gripped the edge of the counter and squeezed her eyes shut.

Her feelings about Blaine had only grown, she realized. The last month had fed them until there was no longer any doubt in her mind that she'd made the stupidest of decisions. It was probably too late now. The sense that she'd placed a barrier between them had grown, and he was observing it.

She heard his step as he returned to the kitchen.

She had to face this, settle this one way or another. She had to know if her hopes should be buried.

"Blaine?" Her voice cracked. She turned to face him and saw him wiping Daphne's drool from the book. To her surprise, he still carried a baby who had become suspiciously wide-awake.

He looked up immediately. "Is something wrong?"

Oh, man, those Irish blue eyes. She licked her lips.

"Well, go on," he said gruffly. "I haven't bitten anyone since I was two, I promise ya."

She squeezed her hands into fists, fearing she was about to experience the worst failure of her life, but knowing she had to take the risk. "You said...you asked... Can we start dating or is it too late?" The words came out on a hurried rush and she stared at him, feeling her heart begin to sink when all he did was look at her.

"Good God, woman," he said presently, "and just what d'ye think we've been doin' these past weeks?"

She froze. His words struck her as if he'd just spun her around and left her dizzy. She closed her eyes briefly, swallowing hard. "Maybe—maybe you should tell me."

A quiet chuckle escaped him. "First, Daffodil's nodding off again, so I think I'd best check her diaper and put her to bed. She woke up on my first try, and I didn't want to leave her to cry. My guess is she'll be waking soon to eat, anyway."

"Usually," Diane agreed, still trying to collect herself. "The fresh air from our walks makes her sleepy and then the book you brought—anyway, she'll be hungry soon. Well, I'm sure I don't have to tell you." Words grew less coherent as her mind struggled to make sense of what he'd said. She was chattering nonsense.

What did she think they'd been doing? Being friends, that was all. Nothing formal. He popped in and popped out whether at work or here. They'd had some great conversations, but he'd never tried to touch her again, not even to hold her hand.

What did she think they'd been doing?

He returned a short while later, smelling pleasantly of baby, and washed his hands at the sink.

"Your tea must be cold," she said quickly. "Let me make you some fresh."

But as she started to rise, he turned and his hand shot out, gripping her forearm gently but firmly. "I don't need tea, Diane. But I think we need a bit of conversation, if that's okay."

The way he held her arm, she could have tugged free with the least effort. He wasn't using force. But she didn't care, because her body was lighting up like the Fourth of July, sparklers spreading anywhere. Time had cured none of her attraction to him. If anything, it felt stronger than ever.

Confident that she wasn't leaving, he sat across from her.

"Now, I understood why you didn't want to date. I told you, I'm not good at that kind of thing. Ya want romance, call an actor—you'll get a better show. But

I understood, and my ham-fisted way of going about it made it seem like this dating thing was all fraught with danger and formality."

She started to open her mouth, but his entire face softened. "Di, be honest. When you heard that, did you kind of panic? Start to feel hemmed in? Like you were going to make a big mistake if you said yes?"

She sighed, lowered her head for a few seconds, then raised it. "I felt confused," she agreed. "I was also…afraid I'd fail."

He nodded. "I reckoned. Merely naming it made it a task you could either mess up or get right. I shouldn't have done that."

"So what have we been doing, Blaine?"

"We've been dating informally. Me dropping by, all that stuff. Bringing dinner over. Little things. And you haven't told me to get lost yet. So yes, if you've changed your mind, I'm agreeable. Seeing more of you would be a pleasure. But we don't have to press it. I don't want to press it. Slow and easy."

He looked away, staring out the window over the sink into the darkening evening. All anyone could see on the glass now was a reflection of this uninspired kitchen.

"I've got me own problems, Di."

She caught her breath. "What do you mean?"

He shrugged one shoulder. "You're afraid of failing, aren't you?"

Sadly, that was something she had no choice but to admit. "Yes. I told you about my mother."

"And your father, to be fair. You said he was a vet?"

She nodded, her insides flip-flopping. "Vietnam. When I was growing up, I sometimes felt…that he was empty inside. That all he wanted was to be left alone. But then there were times—"

"The times that make you keep that chair."

He was looking at her again, so she simply nodded.

"Poor man," he said. "He was the one who failed you, ya know." He held up a hand before she could speak. "I'm not condemning the man. God knows what he went through to leave him such a husk. But it remains, you needed some support to deal with your mother, and you weren't getting it. You felt like a failure because you couldn't please her, and he didn't stand up for you. But he was the failure because he wasn't there when he was needed. Not that it really matters now. Damage is done and all that."

She couldn't speak, had no idea what to say. He was making sense, but she wasn't sure she was ready to accept it. She'd made something of herself, yes, but it was almost in reaction to her mother, not because she was special in any way.

"Anyway, as I was sayin'. I have me own devils to deal with. I told you the story of Ailis, but I rather made light of it. She gave me a lesson and I still have the scars. I've never really let myself care. Too much danger there. But somehow, you're different. Maybe because of Daphne. I don't know how you got under my skin fast. So you're not the only one who's been a bit edgy about this."

He smiled. "I say we date and take it as slow as we need to. Because you're a special woman, Diane Finch, and I'm pretty well hooked. Fair enough?"

"Fair enough," she agreed, her heart beginning to rise like a helium balloon. So she hadn't lost him. And at some point, she hoped he would feel as sure as she was beginning to feel.

Right now, she couldn't ask for anything more.

He extended his hand across the table and she took it, closing her eyes with absolute pleasure as she felt the warmth of his skin once again.

"After we get the daffodil down for the night, or most of it," he said quietly, "I'd like to take you to bed."

"Oh, please," she whispered. "Please."

But then Daphne woke again, her cries sounding cranky. Blaine went to get her, and Diane started their dinner, turning on the oven and scrubbing potato skins.

There was still hope. Thank God. She couldn't believe she had almost thrown away her chance with a man like Blaine Harrigan.

A tear of happiness rolled down her cheek. They'd date. They'd see. And maybe heaven waited in the wings.

Epilogue

Daphne's cries woke Diane, and she looked at the bedside clock. "Three a.m.?" she asked under her breath.

"I'll get her," Blaine said groggily.

"No, I will. It's the cold, I'm sure of it."

But Blaine was already sitting up. "The medicine the doctor gave her isn't helping?"

"Not a whole lot. Besides, who isn't cranky with a cold?"

"Good question," he replied. "I'll check the humidifier then make us something warm to drink. This house is drafty."

"I definitely need to rent a better place," she agreed. Jamming her feet into slippers, wrapping herself in her warmest robe, she slid across the hallway and by the soft glow of the child's bedside lamp, decorated with images of stuffed animals, she found Daphne on her back, blankets kicked off and looking mad as hell.

Diane changed her swiftly, aware of the drafts in the room. That sure didn't make her daughter any happier. She heard Blaine behind her, fumbling with the humidifier, heard him pour more water and probably add more menthol to the cup. The place reeked of menthol right now.

Then she wrapped Daph snugly in a warm blanket and carried her out into the magic that had become her living room.

Blaine didn't believe in half measures. A large Christmas tree, covered with lights and ornaments, filled the front window. She flipped on the lights, and the twinkling and sparkling immediately seized Daph's attention. Her crying subsided to hiccups while Diane wiped her runny nose and wondered if she needed to use the suction bulb to clear her passageways.

At the moment, though, Daph didn't sound totally clogged. Maybe some of that baby ibuprofen for her misery? How she hated not even being able to tell if the girl had a headache or something. She felt warm, but Diane didn't want to undress her again to take her temperature.

Okay, then, she'd see how it went for a while before pulling out the medicine.

She heard the kettle whistle from the kitchen, announcing that tea or hot chocolate would soon arrive. She sat in her dad's old recliner, next to the new one that Blaine had bought. A beautiful Christmassy scene, utterly wasted on Daph.

Well, not entirely, because the girl had become fascinated with the twinkling lights. Her cries steadily diminished until they sounded almost like an afterthought.

Blaine appeared with two mugs of hot chocolate and a bottle. "Do you think she can drink? Or should we aspirate her nose?"

"I'm wondering. Right now I'm not even sure she's hungry."

Daph quieted, still fixated on the lights, evidently liking the display.

"Maybe I should sleep here with her," Diane suggested.

"Fine. I'll join you. If the lights make her happy, we can stay here as long as it takes."

She loved his generosity, his willingness to stay with her, the lack of cranky grumbling of his own as he shuffled back to bed. After all, there was no need for both of them to stay up.

She reached for her hot chocolate.

"Careful."

It was hot, but not too hot to drink. How had he managed that?

"Look," he whispered suddenly. "Me daffodil is nodding off."

"I hope so. She's been so miserable."

"And it's Christmas Eve," he remarked. "I hope next year it's better for her."

"Really? It's Christmas Eve?"

"We passed midnight a few hours ago, darlin'."

She almost laughed. Daph being so sick had evidently cost her her mind. "I forgot."

"I haven't. Think she'll sleep for a bit?"

"She seems comfortable now."

"Then there's something I wanted to do on Christmas Eve, and I don't see any reason to wait until tonight. Seems like with an infant you take your time where you find it."

"Ain't that the truth," she answered wryly.

There were wrapped packages under the tree, mostly toys and clothes for Daphne, but one or two surprises for the two of them. She'd been staring at a huge box with her name on it for days now, wondering what the red-and-gold foil wrapping concealed.

She'd tucked a few things for him under the tree, too. He was a man who didn't seem to want much, so she'd bought him a chamois shirt that nearly matched his eyes and a new set of double-layered gloves. And...well...she hoped he'd understand the Saint Brigid's medal.

He rose now and reached around the back of the tree. In his hand he held a small red box. "I know how you're liking small earrings, studs, right?"

"Right. I love studs because they don't catch on things. And Daph here isn't likely to yank one out of my ear. But that can wait, can't it?"

"No. This is special, and she might only sleep a few minutes, sick as the tyke is."

Then he knelt in front of her and passed her the

red box. "I hope you like my taste. I can always exchange…"

She didn't hear anything else he said, because she opened the box and found an absolutely beautiful ring, a diamond surrounded by tiny emeralds. "Blaine? Blaine?"

"I'm in the way of asking you to marry me, Diane Finch," he said quietly. "And I'm hoping you can answer me before I die of the suspense."

She lifted her gaze from the box and looked into the blue eyes of heaven. "Yes," she whispered, her heart swelling until it felt it would burst. "Oh, yes. I love you so…"

He took the box, removed the ring and slid it onto her left hand. Then he looked straight into her eyes. "I'll be loving you with my last breath, Diane Finch. You are the reason my heart beats. And I wouldn't mind hearing that again."

"I love you," she said more strongly, but any other words were suddenly buried against his shoulder. He wrapped his arm around her, holding her as close as he could without disturbing the baby.

"My heart," he said, and twisted enough to kiss her to the depths of her being.

Daphne decided to protest, but they looked at one another and laughed with joy. Perfect. Everything was perfect, including the cranky baby.

* * * * *

*Don't miss other stories in Rachel Lee's
emotional miniseries,*
CONARD COUNTY: THE NEXT GENERATION,
available now from Harlequin Special Edition:

*A SOLDIER IN CONARD COUNTY
A CONARD COUNTY COURTSHIP
A CONARD COUNTY HOMECOMING
AN UNLIKELY DADDY
A COWBOY FOR CHRISTMAS
A CONARD COUNTY BABY*

COMING NEXT MONTH FROM

HARLEQUIN®

SPECIAL EDITION

Available May 22, 2018

#2623 FORTUNE'S HOMECOMING
The Fortunes of Texas: The Rulebreakers • by Allison Leigh
Celebrity rodeo rider Grayson Fortune is seeking a reprieve from the limelight.
So as his sweet real estate agent, Billie Pemberton, searches to find him the
perfect home, he struggles to keep his mind on business. Grayson is sure he's
not cut out for commitment, but Billie is convinced that love and family are
Grayson's true birthright...

#2624 HER SEVEN-DAY FIANCÉ
Match Made in Haven • by Brenda Harlen
Confirmed bachelor Jason Channing has no intention of putting a ring on any
woman's finger—until Alyssa Cabrera, his too-sexy neighbor, asks him a favor.
But their engagement is just for a week...isn't it?

#2625 THE MAVERICK'S BRIDAL BARGAIN
Montana Mavericks • by Christy Jeffries
Cole Dalton thought letting Vivienne Shuster plan his wedding—to no one—
would work out just fine for both of them. But now not only are they getting
caught up in a lot of lies, they might just be getting caught up in each other!

#2626 COMING HOME TO CRIMSON
Crimson, Colorado • by Michelle Major
Escaping from a cheating fiancé in a "borrowed" car, Sienna Pierce can't think
of anywhere to go but Crimson, the hometown she swore she'd never return
to. When Sheriff Cole Bennet crosses her path, however, Crimson starts to
look a little bit more like home.

#2627 MARRY ME, MAJOR
American Heroes • by Merline Lovelace
Alex needs a husband—fast! Luckily, he doesn't actually need to be around,
so Air Force Major Benjamin Kincaid will do perfectly. That is, until he's
injured—suddenly this marriage of convenience becomes much more than
just a piece of paper...

#2628 THE BALLERINA'S SECRET
Wilde Hearts • by Teri Wilson
With her dream role in her grasp, Tessa needs to focus. But rehearsing with
brooding Julian is making that very difficult. Will she be able to reveal the
insecurities beneath her dancer's poise, or will her secret keep them apart?

HSECNM0518

SPECIAL EXCERPT FROM

H **HARLEQUIN**®

SPECIAL EDITION

*Cole Dalton thought letting Vivienne Shuster
plan his wedding—to no one—would work out just
fine for both of them. But now not only are they getting
caught up in a lot of lies, they might just be getting
caught up in each other!*

*Read on for a sneak preview of
the next **MONTANA MAVERICKS** story,
THE MAVERICK'S BRIDAL BARGAIN
by* **Christy Jeffries***.*

"You're engaged?"

"Of course I'm not engaged." Cole visibly shuddered.
"I'm not even boyfriend material, let alone husband
material."

Confusion quickly replaced her anger and Vivienne
could only stutter, "Wh-why?"

"I guess because I have more important things going
on in my life right now than to cozy up to some female
I'm not interested in and pretend like I give a damn about
all this commitment crap."

"No, I mean why would you need to plan a wedding if
you're not getting married?"

"You said you need to book another client." He rocked
onto the heels of his boots. "Well, I'm your next client."

Vivienne shook her head as if she could jiggle all the
scattered pieces of this puzzle into place. "A client who
has no intention of getting married?"

"Yes. But it's not like your boss would know the difference."

"She might figure it out when no actual marriage takes place. If you're not boyfriend material, then does that mean you don't have a girlfriend? I mean, who would we say you're marrying?"

Okay, so that first question Vivienne threw in for her own clarification. Even though they hadn't exactly kissed, she needed reassurance that she wasn't lusting over some guy who was off-limits.

"Nope, no need for a girlfriend," he said, and she felt some of her apprehension drain. But then he took a couple of steps closer. "We can make something up, but why would it even need to get that far? Look, you just need to buy yourself some time to bring in more business. So you sign me up or whatever you need to do to get your boss off your back, and then after you bring in some more customers—legitimate ones—my fake fiancée will have cold feet and we'll call it off."

If her eyes squinted any more, they'd be squeezed shut. And then she'd miss his normal teasing smirk telling her that he was only kidding. But his jaw was locked into place and the set of his straight mouth looked dead serious.

Don't miss
THE MAVERICK'S BRIDAL BARGAIN
by Christy Jeffries,
available June 2018 wherever
Harlequin® Special Edition books and ebooks are sold.

www.Harlequin.com

— — — — — — ✂ — — — — — —

SHEILA ROBERTS

USA TODAY bestselling author

returns with a brand-new series set on the charming Washington coast.

USA TODAY BESTSELLING AUTHOR

SHEILA ROBERTS

welcome to moonlight harbor

"No one writes emotionally satisfying, warmhearted tales of small-town life quite like Sheila Roberts." —*Booklist*

Once happily married, Jenna Jones is about to turn forty, and this year for her birthday—lucky her—she's getting a divorce. She's barely able to support herself and her teenage daughter, but now her deadbeat artist ex is hitting her up for spousal support…and then spending it on his "other" woman. Still, as her mother always says, every storm brings a rainbow. Then, she gets a very unexpected gift from her great-aunt. Aging Aunt Edie is finding it difficult to keep up her business running The Driftwood Inn, so she invites Jenna to come and run the place. The town is a little more run-down than Jenna remembers, but that's nothing compared to the ramshackle state of The Driftwood Inn. But who knows? With the help of her new friends and a couple of handsome citizens, perhaps that rainbow is on the horizon after all.

Available now, wherever books are sold!